BIRTHDAY

Birthday *is a work of fiction but it deals with many real issues including self-harm and suicidal behaviour. Links to advice and support can be found at the back of the book.*

First published in the UK in 2019 by Usborne Publishing Ltd., Usborne House, 83-85 Saffron Hill, London EC1N 8RT, England. www.usborne.com. Published by arrangement with Rights People, London.

The name Usborne and the devices 🔆🌐 **USBORNE** are Trade Marks of Usborne Publishing Ltd.

alloy**entertainment**

Produced by Alloy Entertainment, LLC.
Candle image by Gabriel San Roman.

A CIP catalogue record for this book is available from the British Library.

ISBN 9781474967419 05384/1 JFM MJJASOND/19
Printed in the UK.

BIRTHDAY

MEREDITH RUSSO

USBORNE

To Mariam, and to every young person
who has the strength to reach out.
To Mom, for surviving.
To Darwin, for no reason except I love you.

THIRTEENTH BIRTHDAY

MORGAN

I'm holding my breath, hovering between wavering sunlight and deep, dark blue, arms twirling while my feet kick up and down, slow as tides. I'm not ready to go back up; too much waits for me above the surface. But I know I can't just float for ever. Life always forces you to move, one way or the other, whether you're bursting into sunlight or swimming down.

The pressure in my chest is soon too much to bear. I hold my arms close and wriggle my whole body, shooting out of the water like a mermaid.

"A minute and a half!" Eric hollers, splashing me in his excitement. I can barely make out his grin as I wipe water from my eyes.

"Told you!" I say. I can see him clearly now. He's small, a few inches shorter than me, with smart, quick, green eyes, shoulder-length blond hair, and a narrow, angled face that swoops down to a point at his chin. "You still wanna take a turn, or do you just give up?"

"Never!" Eric says. He gulps in as much air as he can, holds his nose, and disappears under the water.

I focus on counting out the seconds, light-headed even though I've finally caught my breath. My heart is hammering. I'm gonna tell him when he comes back up. *Ten seconds.* I'm gonna tell him I'm supposed to be a girl, that I can't stand being a boy any more, that I feel like I'm dying a little bit more every day. *Twenty seconds.*

A girl a few years older than me in a red bikini strides by the pool, heading for some distant part of the water park. I catch myself staring at her body, at the shape of it, at how it moves. I realize I've pressed my forearms over my chest and force them back down. There's nothing to cover.

Thirty seconds. Eric's parents and my dad wave from their table near the pool and I wave back. I'm gonna tell Eric, and if he takes it well, I'll tell Dad. It's not that I want to. I have nightmares about making things weird with Eric or adding more stress to Dad's life after everything that's happened, but more and more it feels like I'm gonna explode. I've tried holding it in. Every day I feel a little more numb, a little more monstrous, more afraid I'll look in the mirror and find myself twisting into a tall, hairy man who never gets to turn back.

I've been thinking things that scare me – about not wanting to be alive any more – and I need help. Maybe that help is my best friend, sitting calmly and letting me talk and telling me the way I feel is actually normal, that he's going through it too, that it's part of growing up and we'll pass through it together. Maybe that's my dad finding someone I can talk to, a therapist or something. I don't know, but whatever it is has to happen soon – I'm thirteen, and the bone-twisting terrors of puberty feel close.

Forty seconds. How do you tell someone a secret like this? How do you put it into words?

Fifty seconds, and Eric splashes back into view, arms flailing. "How'd I do?" he rasps.

"Terrible," I say. He splashes in my general direction – he's practically blind without glasses – and I laugh.

"How long was I under?"

"Not even a full minute," I say, splashing him back.

"Whatever," he says, rolling his eyes. "We don't all have your natural talent."

"I run every morning," I say in a sing-song voice. I'd hoped exercising would stop being a part of my life once I quit youth league football, but when your dad's a coach and a PE teacher, it turns out you're stuck. "Work as hard as me and you'll *be* as good as me, scrub." I float on my back, closing my eyes as the sun warms my face and stomach. I take a deep breath. It's easier to imagine saying something when I can't see him. "Hey, Eric?"

"Yeah?"

"If I tell you something," I say, "will you promise to keep it a secret?"

"Dude," Eric says, sounding almost hurt, "like you even need to ask."

"Good," I say. I open my mouth to tell him. My heart hammers. I glance to the side and find my best friend, a person I've known since the day I was born, watching me with open, curious eyes. Staring into them for too long makes my stomach tight in a way I don't like, so I swallow and look back up at the sky.

If my life were a movie, the characters would always know what to say and the boring, disgusting, embarrassing parts would be cut away in the blink of an eye. Indiana Jones would *never* need to have this conversation, and Godzilla doesn't have a gender – it just stomped on cars and blew up buildings with nuclear fire. What a charmed life.

"So?" Eric says. He falls back into the water and rises, blinking his eyes dry. Then he flips his hair out of his face and smoothes it back. My stomach dips. I sink until I'm submerged up to my nose.

"So what is it?"

I blow a stream of bubbles and look away. He wades over and dips his face, smiling and handsome (shut up shut up shut up shut up) into my field of vision. When he sees my face, his smile shifts the tiniest bit, showing confusion and frustration.

"I feel like I'm supposed to be a girl." I say it under the water, the sound coming up garbled. Did Eric make it out?

He rolls his eyes. "Fine, *don't* tell me, weirdo." He didn't hear. I feel sick.

Weirdo.

Eric swims away, clambers over the edge of the pool, and stands, looking down at me as I follow slowly.

Our parents call us over and I imagine saying it now: *I'm really a girl.* It sounds ridiculous. It sounds *weird.*

We run to meet our parents, our wet footprints quickly drying on the hot paving. Carson, Eric's dad, is wearing a "Big Kahuna" T-shirt and long black swimming trunks. He's imposing, over six feet tall, with Eric's same blond hair cut short and sharp green eyes that always seem angry. He used to like me, back when I played football. I even thought of him like an uncle. But ever since I quit, he barely says anything to me, even when I sleep over at their house. I've always thought Eric's mom, Jenny, looked classic, like a starlet from a black-and-white movie. She makes me feel welcome at Eric's house, making sure I have a home-cooked meal whenever I'm over there.

My dad, all rangy limbs and a deep farmer's tan from running around on the football field, gives me a tired smile and slouches back in his chair. Our parents have known one another for as long as Eric and I have been alive. They met at the hospital when we were born, trapped during a freak blizzard – the only September blizzard in Tennessee's history, apparently. During those three autumn days, Eric and I came into the world, and our parents – our families – became friends for life.

Since then, we've done everything together. A shared birthday eventually became a shared everything. For a long time our families were closer to each other than we were to our own uncles, aunts and cousins.

Then Mom died and, not too much later, I quit the football team.

At least we still do our birthday together.

"You boys ready for lunch?" Jenny asks, lifting her oval sunglasses with a smile.

I flinch at her casual use of the word "boys" but try to hide it.

It wasn't always like this; it used to be a dull pain, the ache of a bruise, a faint confusion when school activities split us into boys and girls – but in the last year it's grown unbearable. I might have said something sooner, vaguely remember *wanting* to say something sooner, but I actually used to like football, and I knew instinctively that two kinds of kids weren't allowed to play: girls and sissies. I didn't want to give up something I liked, and I didn't want to be made fun of. Back then, stamping down my confusion was easier, but over time it's turned into something like you'd see in a cartoon, where a character plugs a leak with their finger only for two more leaks to pop out in its place. Feels like it's only a matter of time before the dam bursts right in my face.

"Not yet," Eric says to his mom as he twists out his hair. "I want to hit the Vortex."

Our white-and-blue birthday cake sits at the centre of the table. It says *Happy birthday, boys!* in red icing, so even if grocery store cakes *didn't* taste like trash compared to Mom's baking, I still wouldn't want to eat it. I nod along with Eric and try to look like I'm excited about the Vortex too.

"Okay," Dad says, starting to rise. "I'll come with you."

"Hey, hey, Tyler. They're thirteen now," Carson says, leaning back and sipping his Coke. "Maybe it's time to let out the reins a little bit."

"Maybe you're right," Dad says, scratching his cheek. He looks at me, giving me an *are you okay?* expression.

Dad used to let me run around like a crazy person, used to say it was good for boys to scuff their knees. But then Mom got sick, and then she got sicker, and a year ago she was gone, and ever since it feels like he's either always on the football field, gone, or trying to put a leash around my neck. It's like we're both treading water around each other, unsure of how to act without her.

I let my hair fall into my face. It's always easier to view the world through the veil of my hair. I turn, and with my eyes locked on Eric we jog away from the pool towards the main walkway, closer to the looming shadow of the Vortex.

"You okay?" Eric asks as we get in line and start to mount the wrought-iron stairs.

"I'm fine," I say.

I have to tell him. I *have* to tell him.

"Is it because you're scared of heights?" Eric asks.

I look around and we're almost to the top now. A breeze whips Eric's hair. A cloud of starlings wheels above the park like a school of fish.

"I'm not scared of heights," I say, rolling my eyes. "I'm not scared of anything."

What a lie.

"Then why are you acting weird?"

"I'm not," I say. I look down at my feet and at the dizzying vista visible through the gaps in the wrought iron.

Eric gives me a look like he doesn't believe me, but before he can say anything else, we're on the top platform with the dark, open mouth of the waterslide beckoning. An attendant guides us to a small, yellow inflatable raft and instructs us to hold onto the handles, not to stand up, not to leave the raft, not to do any of the stupid things teenage boys apparently do, which reminds me for the millionth time: I'm a teenage boy now. It's official. I feel sick.

"Ready?" the attendant asks us.

I nod. Eric shoots his arms in the air and hollers.

The attendant laughs, nudges the raft with a sandalled

foot, and suddenly we're wrapped up in dark, screaming motion. The raft careens through the tube, riding so high on the walls whenever we turn that it feels like we might go flying. Eric laughs manically, shielding his face with his arms as water sprays us. I laugh too. The excitement builds and builds, eclipsing every other emotion, until finally I yell into the darkness: "Eric! I want to be a girl!"

"All right!" Eric shouts. And I can't believe it.

All right? All right. He said all right.

I just let my body laugh, let the laughter twist and erupt out of me like poison flowing out of a wound, and suddenly I feel weightless. A circle of light appears, blinding at first, expanding at the speed of sound, and then we're bathed in sunshine, tumbling, flipping over the raft into the pool below.

I'm the first to the surface. I tread in place for a moment, ignoring the rushing water, the screaming children, the music blaring over the park's PA. *I told him. I told him. It's all right.*

Eric comes up a moment later, flailing and gasping for air, his eyes hidden behind a wet sheet of curly hair. I grab his arm and drag him to shallow water, sputtering and laughing at the same time.

"That was rad!"

"It was awesome!" I say, splashing as my arms fly into the air.

All right. All right. He said *all right.*

15

"What'd you say in there?" he asks me, panting. "I couldn't hear."

"Oh," I say, my insides tightening up.

He didn't hear.

He doesn't know.

I'd had a vision as I'd gone down the waterslide, or a cloud of competing visions, all paradise in their way: Eric telling me I'm normal, Eric telling me I'm not normal but he understands and he'll still talk to me and keep my secret, and distantly, but shining gold and warm, a vision of myself as a girl, walking happily next to him at school as if it's the most normal thing in the world. The visions flicker out like heat ripples on tarmac.

My stomach keeps twisting, but it's useless to try to stop it.

I slowly wade my way out of the pool. Everything's spinning. I run to the nearest trash can, brace my hands on the rim, and throw up.

ERIC

The birthday cake sits in my lap, bouncing with each bump on the interstate. One side has been carved away, and most of it is behind us in the water park trash can. Morgan tried eating some, claiming he was okay, only to throw up again, and the sight – and smell – cost the rest of us our appetites. So we all decided it was time to go home.

I watch I-75 roll past, carrying us north from Georgia back into Tennessee. My cheeks and shoulders glow with what will probably be sunburn, but feels warm and nice for now. My older brother, Peyton, sulks in the seat next to me. Apparently he met some girls who were willing to talk to him and Morgan puking interrupted this once-in-a-lifetime miracle. Dad bobs his head to Johnny Cash on the classic country station while Mom looks totally lost in the latest Patricia Cornwell novel. I have a book in my backpack, the story of Radiohead, or I could relisten to the Mountain Goats album *Tallahassee*, but I don't really feel like reading or even listening to music.

It's hard to focus on anything really. I just keep thinking about what was up with Morgan today, and what his big secret was. He's been kind of…far away ever since his mom died. It's selfish, and I want to be there for him, but it's more and more like he's never present. He was always quiet and kind of thoughtful, more of a listener than a talker, unless something made made him mad, but nowadays I'm lucky if I can get him to do more than grunt and chew his thumbnail in response to half the things I say. Who knew you could feel lonely with someone right beside you?

Morgan's been my best friend since for ever. His mom taught both of us to read from the same copy of *Go Dog Go*. He told me the moment he figured out Santa wasn't real. I joined the junior football team, even though I hated football, because Morgan was the quarterback. I even asked to be left tackle on the offensive line because taking hits for my friend felt like the most natural thing in the world.

We've spent our summers climbing trees, wandering dry creek beds, and lying in fields watching clouds scud by. We've slept in the same bed every Friday or Saturday night since preschool, talking until late into the night about music (my Mountain Goats phase was preceded by a two-month obsession with Neutral Milk Hotel's *In the*

Aeroplane Over the Sea, and Morgan's managed to turn me onto some of the metal bands he's into, like Atreyu, and, if he's in the right mood, all the hippie girl music like Kate Bush and Tori Amos that his mom loved and he doesn't mind admitting he loves too), movies (*Almost Famous* for me and a tie between *Mulan* and *The Royal Tenenbaums* for him), and *everything* else. We used to share everything.

And then, at the start of the summer, I remember I noticed a girl in a different way. I was riding my bike to Morgan's house, and as I sped through his trailer park, I passed a girl I vaguely recognized as the older sister of someone in our class – a high schooler, in a one-piece bathing suit and cut-off shorts, and she was standing in a kiddie pool spraying the mud off her legs with a garden hose. I'd always thought girls were pretty before, and I'd sort of liked being around them sometimes, but watching this older girl bathing was the key in the lock that turned everything else on.

I tried bringing it up with Morgan and for the first time in our whole lives he'd just stonewalled me, said he didn't want to talk about that, and turned over to go to sleep. It seemed so minor, *would* be so minor for anyone else, but we've never been like that. Never.

I wish I could talk to him about why everything felt so weird today, wish I knew what his secret was. I'm not stupid. I know what it *probably* is. I've never met a gay person (that I know of), but I'll support Morgan no matter what he tells me. He *must* know that. He *must* know I would stick with him and keep his secret, right?

"Awful quiet back there," Mom says. I look up to see her red eyebrows raised and a faint, curious smile on her lips.

"He's thinking about *boys*," Peyton says, with an exaggerated lisp. I lean back and kick at him, but he blocks and retaliates with a knuckle pop in my bicep. I yelp and rub my arm. Peyton laughs.

Dad and Mom don't notice or don't much care that Peyton just told the car I was gay, which makes me think about Morgan again. *I'm* not gay, so I've never really thought about it, but guys around here really do throw that word around like it's nothing. If I were gay and I heard everyone around me constantly calling everything they don't like gay and yelling "Fag!" at the drop of a hat, maybe that would make it hard to come out even to people I care about.

"Did you enjoy your birthday?" Mom asks me once I've stopped wincing.

"It was okay, I guess," I say, swallowing and looking down at the cake. I worry sometimes that I'm ungrateful, because I know we have a lot of money compared to other families in Thebes, but I don't think they should have gotten us a birthday cake this year. There was just no way it would compare with what Morgan's mom, Donna, used to make. Even a cookie cake would have been a better choice.

"If you wanted to stay, all you had to do was say so," Mom says.

"No," I say. I flatten a palm against the plastic dish covering the icing. "It would have been weird without Morgan." Mom gives me a sad smile – I feel like she gives me more and more of them every day.

"Everything's weirder *with* Morgan," Dad says from the driver's seat. Peyton snorts beside me. The two of them share a look in the rear-view mirror. Mom clears her throat and makes a point of noisily turning the page in her book, but Dad ignores her.

"What do you mean?" I ask, but Dad just drums his fingers.

"Thought he'd have grown out of it by now, that's all."

"Guys…" Mom says, but I can't help but push on.

"Grown out of what?" I ask as if I don't know. I'm *thirteen*, I'm not a little kid, but adults still act like I don't know anything.

"Being a faggot," Peyton mutters. I feel heat rising in my cheeks. There it is.

Mom shoots Peyton a look. "Peyton, please."

There's a moment of silence, but it doesn't last. In my experience guys like Peyton and Dad are sort of like sharks: one drop of blood in the water puts them into a frenzy. Dad runs his fingers through his hair and glances at me in the rear-view mirror. "Used to be football kept him a little tough. But come on, Eric, the boy's always been kind of a sissy."

"What?" I say. "No, he's not. What the hell?" Maybe Morgan can be a little girly sometimes, but he was the best player in junior *and* youth league.

"*Language*," Mom says.

"Hey, Dad," Peyton says. He leans forward, grinning like a coyote. "Hey. Remember when Morgan threw that shit fit –" I wait for Mom to correct his language, but it doesn't come – "'cause his parents wouldn't let him dress up as that Chinese cartoon girl for Halloween?"

Dad barks out a laugh and slaps the steering wheel. All I can think of is how that was two years ago, when Morgan had just gotten the news about his mom's cancer. I can only guess that he probably didn't know how to feel about anything.

"It wasn't a *girl*," I say. "It was Mulan's *male* soldier costume, so if anything he was—"

"God, who cares about that stupid cartoon, nerd?" Peyton says. "He cried over Halloween either way. Like a girl."

"All right, all right," Dad says, but there's laughter in his voice. The sound makes my skin crawl. "All I'm saying is that Tyler needs to show the kid how to be a man. He's a goddamn football coach – he's gotta whip that boy back into shape."

Heat flares into my face. I tuck my hands into my pockets so Peyton can't see that they're shaking. I rest my forehead against the window and focus on the glass's coolness. *Morgan* always knows how to deal with Peyton. I wish I could just cut loose like he does, snap off some gut punch of an insult, or scream and kick something over, but all I can ever seem to do is fold my hands under my arms and stay quiet. And yet somehow *Morgan's* the "sissy"?

Peyton jabs me in the shoulder. "What's wrong? Is widdle baby Eric upset?"

"Go fuck yourself," I say through clenched teeth. What do you know? I guess I *did* have it in me.

Mom snaps her head around. "*Language!*"

"Fine!" I say.

"Don't raise your voice at your mother!" Dad yells.

"Yes, sir," I say. I want to talk back, but making Dad angry is a one-way ticket to grounded.

A long, rumbling silence passes, and just when I've started to calm down, an ad for Dad's car dealership, the place every McKinley son is doomed to work if he can't pay his own way through college, comes on the radio. He turns up the volume.

Dad started the business straight out of high school and it's his pride and joy. Sometimes I think he loves those stupid cars more than our whole family put together. He turns the volume up with a "Whoop!" and sings along to the hokey jingle, and my mom and Peyton join in.

23

Dad catches my eye in the rear-view mirror. I stare back.

I push my lips together and start to hum.

He smiles at me, his mouth spreading wide, almost smug, but I notice his eyes don't crinkle up. I smile back as long as I can manage and turn my gaze back to the road.

It's still a long way home from here.

MORGAN

"Think you'll need to see a doctor?" Dad asks. He cranks his window down and props his elbows on the truck's steering wheel. I pause my Atreyu song and give him my attention. Even though I don't want to talk to anyone right now, it's been so hard getting anything real from him since Mom died that I can't help noticing when he takes any noticeable interest besides sporadically babying me.

Do I need to see a doctor? I think of the internet searches and forum posts I've read about this thing that's wrong with me, about the surgeries and hormones I might need, or want, or…the whole thing is so confusing. But that's not what Dad's asking about. He's just worried that I threw up. I'm tempted to tell him, to let it explode from me, but then my eyes drift to his face and I see how tired he is all the time, how he almost never sleeps, how he takes odd jobs on top of coaching. I can't add more to that. I can't tell him I should be his daughter.

"No," I say. I rub my stomach and shake my head. "Just too much gas station food, I guess. I feel better now."

He grunts in acknowledgement. I put one of my headphones back in, watch the road drift by, and try not to think about how Eric couldn't hear me at the water park, and how my secret is still safe, and how Eric looked cute without a shirt on, and how I wish I didn't even think that. It had been a mistake to think to tell him. I push the truth down. Bury it. Stick a grave marker on top. What's one more year of life as a boy?

My thoughts drift to Mom and I wonder if I would have been able to tell her how I felt wrong in my own body, if she would have understood. Mom was sensitive, and soft-spoken, and always kind – even to people I could tell she didn't like. I think she would have loved me no matter what.

I guess I'll never know.

But I can hope.

We pass under the highway overpass that marks the entrance to Thebes, to home. Thebes is a sleepy little mountain town nestled between Knoxville and Nashville. It's the type of place where the only noteworthy things to do are drive through or drive away. We aren't rich on Dad's coaching salary, but it feels like we have a fortune compared to some kids at my school.

Dad told me once that there used to be a coal mine and a couple of factories in Thebes, that the highway got enough traffic before I-40 was put in that there were more restaurants and hotels than any local could visit. There were jobs.

Without the mine and the factories, Thebes is just a Walmart and a chicken processing plant and a bunch of big, empty buildings with boards over some windows and shattered glass in the rest. Worse than the cracked paving and drooping, forgotten telephone poles are the ghosts lurking everywhere I look.

There's the movie theatre Mom took me to every other Sunday as our special ritual. I still remember watching *Mulan* beside her and feeling a quiet thrill of pleasure. And although I was only five, even then I suspected I wasn't supposed to say anything about how cool it was that a girl could also be a boy.

We drive past the field where my junior league played, where other kids' parents cheered and clapped and made me feel special, where boys my age smiled when they saw me – instead of slapping books out of my hands and kicking my legs when no one was watching like they do now.

There's Federal Park with the stream running through it, the stream you *can't* drink from, shimmering and iridescent with run-off from one of the old mines. Eric's family and mine would cook out here in the summers, but we haven't in the past couple of years. It wouldn't be the same without Mom's potato salad, and her recipe book has gone missing – not that Dad or I would even know where to start with cooking. We mainly subsist on frozen dinners and takeout.

We pass Burke's Funeral Home, a converted white plantation house where I sat in the parking lot and, for the first but definitely not the last time, felt so apocalyptically sad and angry that I couldn't stop crying. There's Oak County High School, where I'll have to go next year, every part of it dilapidated and crumbling except the football field, which always looks like someone just went over every inch of the bleachers and lights with a toothbrush.

It's late afternoon, darkening into evening, when we finally pull into our trailer park. I hop down from the truck without saying anything, shuffle inside, and head straight to the hall closet. I don't hear Dad come after me. He knows what I'm up to.

After some digging, I find the small cardboard box labelled MORGAN'S BABY TAPES. I crawl under a rack of Dad's dress shirts, lift the lid, and read the looping, feminine handwriting on the tapes' spines. Mostly they're old home movies on VHS, but there are two smaller handycam tapes Mom made just before she passed – she'd wanted to leave a birthday present for me. Her plan was that she'd make a video for every year she would miss. I think she wanted to go all the way from my twelfth up to my eighteenth birthday, but then everything happened so fast. We had less than a year from a diagnosis to the funeral. In the end she only made these two birthday tapes for me.

I remember last September. It was a month after my twelfth birthday that I finally worked up the nerve to watch the first birthday tape. She hadn't been gone that long and listening to her voice felt like water after a long day in the heat. I watched her speak to me over and over, until the tape started to decay, and it took all my willpower not to immediately watch the next one – the last one. Now, a year later, I'm glad I waited.

I find the tape labelled 13TH BIRTHDAY, pull it out, shut the closet door behind me, and walk to my bedroom. I can hear Dad in the small kitchen, listening to Merle Haggard and pouring whiskey over ice cubes while he thaws a pair of steaks.

I close my door behind me and jam a towel in the space under it. With shaking hands, I slip the handycam tape into the VHS-sized adapter and sit straight-backed as the video begins. There's a moment of static and then the screen glows blue and green. I recognize our old apartment's balcony. Dad and I moved the summer after …everything. He realized we couldn't make rent on just his salary. It didn't feel like home without Mom anyway.

Pots of herbs and tomatoes hang off the railing and flowering vines climb up to the roof. In the midst of all this greenery sits my mom, so much skinnier than I want to remember her. A floral scarf conceals her bald head. She wears another scarf around her shoulders and a long-sleeved cardigan even though it's obviously a warm spring day. She has the same cheekbones as me, the same high eyebrows, the same large eyes that seem to fill up her face.

"Hello, Morgan," she says. I can hear blue jays singing.

"Hi, Mom," I whisper.

"Happy thirteenth birthday!" she says, her eyes wrinkling when her smile widens.

"Thanks, Mom."

"Thirteen…" she says again. Her smile turns sad. "I can't believe you're a teenager now. That a whole year has passed." She gives a soft, tired sigh. "We just picked you up from your grandma's house and she says you ran laps around the backyard all afternoon." I smile. "Are you still on Dad's football team?" No. I quit because my body started making me feel sick, because I felt too sad to go to practice, because little parts of what's wrong with me kept slipping through.

I squeeze my eyes shut to try and push those memories away. Dad shouting at me and making me "get in there" with the other boys. Eric bringing guys like Nate and Chud from the team to hang out with us.

"I hope so," Mom goes on. "You've always been so graceful on the field, all legs and speed, though Lord knows I barely even learned the difference between a blitz and a bootleg.

"Well," Mom says, "whatever you're interested in nowadays, I'm sure you're after it like a creature possessed." She looks up out of the frame and shakes her head a little. "You've always been so obsessive over the things you care about. It's one of your best and worst qualities, I think."

"Yeah, Mom. You're right," I say, my voice quaking just a little. What I don't tell her is that since quitting football I've been making secret movies with our old handycam for over a year now. I haven't wanted Dad to find out. He'd probably think it's a waste of time and a waste of money on tapes, which I guess it is. And how would I even tell him? "So, Dad, I quit football, but what I really want to do is make it in *Hollywood*!" I feel ridiculous and sad even thinking it. I already know what he'd say. "You don't escape a place like this on dreams and luck. I can't pay to send you to college. You want out of this town? You do it with football, not movies."

No point having a conversation if I already know how it ends.

Through the door, I hear steak sizzling and picture Dad, tired and half awake, pushing the meat around in a skillet, making a big dinner for the two of us.

I pull my attention back to the video and see the back of a small head – my head, two-ish years ago – enter the frame from the left.

"Mom?" eleven-year-old me asks. "What are you doing?"

I lick my lips and quickly squeeze my eyes shut. I remember this moment. I remember waking up and following my mom's voice out to the balcony. I remember seeing her in front of the camera, smiling but sad, and feeling like I was trespassing on something grown-up. In that moment, I was frustrated with her for being sick, and now the guilt of that feeling runs through me like a fever.

"Making a birthday present for when you're older," she says, leaning down to kiss me on the forehead. "Whatever you need, could you go ask your father?"

"Okaaaaaaay…" little me says and leaves the frame again. Mom's eyes come back up to mine.

"You were such a wonderful child," she says quietly, her voice fading. She looks more and more tired every minute that I watch her. "And I'm so glad I got to know you before…" She gives a longer sigh this time. "For all the things I don't know about thirteen-year-old Morgan, I do know you must be growing into a fine young man." My shoulders slump at that. "Are you still friends with Eric?" she says. She cocks her head, giving me time to answer. But I can't. The memory of what happened at the water park today comes charging back. A wave of disgust with myself rolls over my skin.

Mom starts to speak again. "Keep that boy close. I do my best not to be superstitious, but you two need each other." There's a long silence where she just looks into the camera and smiles. "I need to rest now, okay?"

"Okay," I say, and now my eyes are burning.

"Happy birthday, baby," she says, leaning towards the camera. "I love you."

"Love you too," I say, feeling off-centre.

And then the screen is blank.

I let the fuzzy black-and-white static fill the room as I sit back on my heels. After a bit, the tape runs out and ejects itself. I crawl forward, push the VHS back in, rewind it, and watch it again. There's a pressure behind my eyes, a tightness in my throat, a heat climbing up my chest. I know I need to cry, and I know I'll probably feel better if I do, but more and more lately I just can't. More and more my feelings end up festering inside me. I can't let go, can't release.

I always thought boys cried less because they...*we* got yelled at for it, but now the tears won't come even when I want them. I wonder if maybe I just can't cry any more, if maybe growing up means testosterone is running through my body like an invading army, butchering and burning everything tender.

I watch the video again and then again, my lips eventually moving in sync with Mom's. I try to memorize everything she said, to imagine a scene of us sitting together on the balcony, talking. When the VHS ends for the fifth time, I sit and stare at nothing for a while until Dad's voice breaks the quiet. "Dinner's ready!" he calls.

I go into the kitchen, take one look at the overdone steak and his tired, bloodshot eyes, and don't feel the slightest bit hungry. We eat on the couch, our plates in our laps, watching recorded SEC games in silence. Dad's schedule always leaves him behind on watching college and professional football, and Sunday is his day to catch up. I push a glob of mashed potatoes around my plate and stare into space, away from the players on the screen.

"Oh, hey," Dad says. "It's your birthday. We don't have to watch this, we can—"

"It's fine," I say. "How're the Vols doing this season?"

"Pretty good all told," Dad says, and things feel normal for just a moment. He leans back, crosses his legs, and scratches his chin thoughtfully. "I heard this game against Florida don't end well though, but that ain't exactly *new*."

"Right," I say.

"I still say our main rivalry's with them and not with Alabama."

"Yeah. How's Isaac doing there?" I say. Eric's oldest brother wouldn't have been caught dead at the water park with us today even though he's in town for the weekend, and I guess I can't blame him. He's a lot older.

"Great for a college freshman," Dad says. He pretends to buff his nails on his shirt and cracks a smug smile. "Still waiting on my thank-you letter from Coach Fulmer for the work I put into that boy."

"Don't hold your breath," I joke.

"Right," Dad says. He shakes his head, then looks thoughtful. "So, hey, Eric's gonna try for junior varsity next year. He tell you that?"

"Yeah," I say. "He did."

"You're still the fastest kid at that school. If we put in a little work, hit the weight room, ran some drills, I could probably get you in with him."

I know, in my brain, that this is his way of trying to spend time with me. Football is the beating heart of our town – football scholarships get kids out of Thebes, and even players who don't get recruited, who spend the rest of their lives stuck here, get to look back fondly on the time when they were champions.

This town expects a lot of Dad – to make these heroes, to put Thebes on the map. I never realized just how much time Dad spent coaching until I quit playing and noticed I only saw him in the morning, an hour or so at night, and half of every Sunday. Sometimes I think any of the boys on the team would be a better *son* than me. At least they wouldn't be a walking disappointment. They wouldn't remind him what he's lost every time he looks at them.

But the more he asks me to rejoin the team the more I think *I'm so tired of this conversation.*

"No," I say. "I don't want to play football any more, Dad."

"Okay," he says. He takes a long breath and runs his hand down his face. "I...sorry. Just trying to help."

The pressure comes back to my throat.

He's floundering too. But he's trying. And I know he loves me and he's all I have – besides Eric.

"I know," I whisper.

"How was the video?" he says.

"Good," I say. "It was good. Nice."

"That's good," Dad says.

I start to say more, to tell him how even though it hurts to see her in the videos, it's still a relief, because sometimes I stare at the ceiling at night and can't remember exactly what she looked like in motion and alive, how she smelled, how she sounded. I want to tell him how hurting like this is better than forgetting her.

But we've only really talked much about her once since the funeral. I'd found her college sketchbook while we were moving and Dad had sat with me, telling me what he remembered about each of her amazingly lifelike drawings. I remember his voice trembling, and when we reached a page near the middle, there was a figure who was clearly a younger Dad seated on a log, a baseball cap high on his forehead, his eyes squinting at something off the page while he pulled on a cigarette. She'd managed to capture Dad's thoughtfulness with nothing but a pencil, and under it she'd written, by way of a title, "My Future Husband".

Dad had held it together through every night at the hospital, through the final talk with the doctor, and even through the funeral. But something about this drawing opened the dam and he started sobbing. He locked himself in his bedroom and cried for almost an hour, and when he came back, neither of us said anything. I'd never seen him cry before and I don't think I could stand to see it again.

So, we don't talk about her, at least not directly.

I spear some broccoli, think about putting it in my mouth, and then drop it in the mashed potatoes.

We go quiet and keep watching the game for a little while. It's close, but the Vols are clearly struggling and then, twenty-one to twenty-two in Florida's favour, the Gators' defence manages to run down the clock. Dad groans and rubs his temples. I use the distraction to get up and dump my mostly untouched plate in the trash.

"There's always next season," I say.

"Can't think like that when you're a coach," he says.

"I guess." I stand still. "Thanks for dinner."

"Of course. Birthday and all. I know it's not what it used to be…"

It's been two years since we had a birthday dinner like that. Mom and Jenny used to cook a huge dinner for all of us. Mom would make dessert – she was such a good baker that now pastries and cakes from the grocery store taste awful in comparison. Eric's oldest brother, Isaac, still lived at home. Peyton wasn't as mean. Mom was alive and healthy.

"It's fine," I say. "It was good."

If Dad noticed I didn't eat anything, he doesn't show it, just nods and smiles as I step outside. He'll probably leave soon to organize equipment or whatever a coach does when he doesn't want to be at home, leaving me to come up with a way to pass the time.

I let the screen door bang behind me and squat to sit on the front steps of our trailer. Three long-haired kids scream and splash in a plastic pool across the lane while their aunt, a round older woman with a grey ponytail and horn-rimmed glasses, watches them and works through a pack of Camels. The smell of smoke, grease and barbecue sauce wafts on the breeze.

Distantly, so faint it could almost be a thought, I hear a thrum of an acoustic guitar.

Eric. I wonder if he's playing the guitar Mom gave him right now? It's hard to say why, but for some reason I'm sure he is, and if she's capable of hearing him, I know she must be happy. The thought only makes me more miserable.

I kick at the pebbles at my feet and stub my toe with a sharp intake of breath. *I hate you*, I hiss at that stupid rock. I hate this trailer park *almost* as much as I hated living in the apartment that reminded me of Mom every minute of every day. I hate it for having no permanence, and I hate it for not being my home, and I hate that there is no home to go back to any more.

Closing my eyes, I put in my headphones, and let myself drift away to anywhere but here. I pull my knees to my chest, trying to become so small that I disappear.

ERIC

The fireflies are out. I'm sitting on our back porch, watching them twinkle and twirl, while I absent-mindedly play my guitar. I finger an F chord, which was the hardest one to get right when I was first learning. Now it's not too bad.

The guitar was my last birthday present from Morgan's family before Donna died, this and a songbook with tabs for popular nineties rock songs from the McKay's in Knoxville. They were both from the Gardners collectively, but I know that Donna picked them out. She always said I had long fingers, perfect for playing music, and it would be a shame to let them go to waste. I owe her for seeing that such a thing existed in me – that my hands can do something besides catch a football. It's also thanks to her that my taste in music isn't just songs that are about trucks, and that the country I *do* listen to leans more towards

My Morning Jacket and Old Crow Medicine Show than Garth Brooks. I'd be lying, though, if I said I don't still enjoy the *occasional* stadium song about a really nice truck.

I play a G minor. Hold it.

B flat major 7 chord.

Strum.

I switch back and forth between the chords, liking the way the strings make my fingers ache. Aching is good. Aching means they're getting stronger.

A lawnmower buzzes to life and my oldest brother, Isaac, pushes it around the corner into the backyard, sending the fireflies floating off. I watch him work for a little while, setting my guitar aside. Isaac is huge, a carbon copy of Dad when he was in high school. All abs and thick biceps and square jaw, but with Mom's dark red hair. He's nineteen now, at the University of Tennessee in Knoxville on a football scholarship. He came home for my birthday, but I know it was mostly to see his girlfriend, since he skipped out on the water park. Isaac stops halfway through the yard, kills the mower, and wipes his forehead. He smiles when he notices me sitting there, watching him.

"Stay there, birthday boy." He strides across the yard, climbs the porch steps, and heads into the kitchen. Sometimes Isaac's kind of a jerk, though not in the same way as Peyton. My birthday is the only time Isaac can be counted on to be in Good Brother mode, and most of the time even Peyton doesn't show his ass. Though Morgan did give Peyton a bloody nose once when we were eight and he was eleven. Peyton kicked a controller out of Morgan's hand when he'd lost too many times at Tekken and Morgan leaped across the couch and busted his nose with one wild punch. That's the Morgan I know – the kid who's gonna dish it back – not the one like today, who shut down and seemed so off.

Isaac comes back out a moment later with two Coronas. "Here."

"Won't we get in trouble?" I say. I take the bottle in both hands. It's ice cold and sweats against my palms.

"I won't tell if you won't," Isaac says, kicking his feet up on the wicker table and taking a swig of beer. "Besides, it's your thirteenth birthday. You're a man now!"

"Am I?" I take a sip of the beer and don't hate it like I thought I might. It's mellow and bubbly, like a soda, but savoury instead of sweet.

"My voice hasn't even dropped yet," I say, taking another, longer sip. By way of example, I put the beer down and finger the opening riff to "Come As You Are", the first part of the book I ever mastered, and sing the opening lines, intentionally making my voice squeak and crack even more than it normally does.

"Details," he says, laughing and waving his hand. "So, how's it feel? Thirteen?"

"It feels…okay," I say. I run my foot through the grass.

42

"I guess I'm worried everything's changing and I can't stop it."

"Like what?" Isaac says. He waggles his eyebrows. "Girls giving you that *special feeling* yet?"

I lean back and frown, while he laughs at my expression. "I guess? I don't know. I'm just worried about Morgan. It feels like we're growing apart, and…" I take another sip of beer to stop myself from saying anything else.

"Eh, you won't care so much when high school starts," Isaac says. "Sure, you need to make time for your boys, but, I don't know, you talk about him like he's your girlfriend. Honestly even if he *was* your girlfriend I'd think you were pretty whipped."

I try to tell myself Isaac means well, but he sounds too much like Dad and Peyton did in the car, and maybe that's not surprising. Of my two older brothers, I like Isaac more, but it feels sometimes like he has a hard time thinking of girls as people, or understanding why someone would care about anything other than sports.

"Cool talk," I say.

He shrugs and rolls his eyes. "You'll thank me later," he says, then gets up again to finish mowing the lawn, scaring off the fireflies, probably for good.

I leave my beer half-finished on the porch, figuring everyone will assume it's Isaac's, and head inside.

That's when I notice the half-eaten birthday cake on the counter and get an idea. I fish for some Tupperware and lift the plastic lids, cut off two big pieces of cake, seal them up, and carry them to the living room where I left my backpack.

"Finally!" Peyton says, looking down from the top of the stairs. "Cake time!"

"It's not for you!" I say with a glare.

Mom and Dad look up from the TV as I make my way to the front door.

"I'm going out," I say.

"Not this late you're not," Dad says.

"I need to see Morgan." I swallow hard. I can't think of a time I've ever defied my parents. Maybe it's the beer.

"Morgan's got a stomach bug," Mom says. "He needs to be left alone. And besides, you'll see him at school."

"No," I say. I shake my head. "I need to see him now."

They start to say something else, but I'm out the door and jogging for the garage before they can get a word in. I hear the front door open behind me, but I'm already on my bike, pedalling furiously down the street.

Morgan's trailer is twenty minutes away by bike, and mostly uphill through neighbourhoods Dad calls rough, trashy, and other things I don't like repeating even in my own head. People wave at me from trailer stoops, and from apartment balconies, and from corners near burned-out buildings. They pass cigarettes back and forth and watch cars pass by.

It's clear Thebes has seen better times, and I know I'm

lucky to have a family with money, but I hope I never let any of that distract me from the beauty hiding in everything – the light through the clouds, the shadows on the mountains, and the smiles of people who might not be perfect, who have every reason to be miserable, but still find small ways to be kind to each other every day. Dad says I'm naïve, and when he's in a bad mood Morgan says I would feel different if I were poor, and maybe both of them are right.

When I finally arrive at Morgan's trailer park I'm drenched in sweat and condensation from the gathering mist. I lean against the darkened leasing office for a second before making the final climb to Morgan's lot, where I find him sitting on his stoop in a baggy hoodie, his knees pulled up to his chin, his eyes locked somewhere far off. The crunch of my bike in his gravel driveway draws his attention and for a moment his wide, dark-rimmed eyes pin me to the ground.

"Hey," he says. His tone is flat and I can't tell if it's because he's sad or because he doesn't want to see me. It's so hard to imagine either of us not wanting to see the other, but who knows what's going on in his head lately?

"Hey," I say, and suddenly feel stupid. "I brought cake." I pat my backpack. He leads me inside and I melt into the couch, my T-shirt sticking to my skin. There's no sign of his dad, so he must have come up with an excuse to be at work.

Morgan just watches me, head tilted. "That's it?" he asks. Of course, there's more I want to ask him: how come things have been weird lately? Are you gay? Are we going to be friends for ever? Is it weird that I'm worried about all that? But instead, I don't say anything at all.

I take out the Tupperware containers and drop them on the coffee table. "Let's feast!" I say.

"You're so weird," Morgan finally replies, and it stings, even though I know he doesn't mean it the way my brothers do. He smiles and shakes his head, then disappears into the small kitchen. He returns with two forks, and sits beside me on the couch.

"*I'm* weird?" I say through a mouthful of cake. "You should have seen yourself today."

"I don't know what you mean," Morgan says. His expression turns blank. But I know him. I know when he's actually chill and when he's faking it.

"What was it you tried to tell me earlier?" I say. He shoves cake in his mouth to avoid talking and hunches his shoulders. "You can tell me."

"It's nothing," Morgan says. He wipes frosting from his lips and looks away.

"You can tell me if…" I start, and I want to finish with, "if you're gay," but it feels like the wrong thing to say. And as much as I think that's maybe Morgan's secret, part of me also thinks that maybe I'm wrong. Honestly, for every girly thing Morgan does, I can think of something gross

46

or rowdy to balance it out. Sometimes he lip-syncs to Mariah Carey with a hairbrush as a mic, but sometimes he falls off his bike and barely notices that he's skinned his whole leg. Sometimes he sits with his legs crossed and flips his hair, but sometimes he farts when I sleep over at his house and laughs so hard about it he can't breathe. We've only talked about girls the one time, and he wasn't interested, but we spend so much time together I think I would have noticed him looking at guys.

To me, Morgan is just Morgan, like he's always been, but sadder and more distant every day. If he *is* gay, then I know it could be really good for him to hear that it's okay. But if he isn't, then what if I accidentally offend him? I really just want to tell him it's going to be fine, whatever it is.

Morgan takes a deep breath, like he's thinking about something, squares his shoulders, and then deflates again. "I was just stressed about watching this year's birthday tape," he says. "It's just…hard."

Morgan wipes at his nose and I shut my eyes tight, mad at myself. Of course. I should have known it was his mom.

He rests his forehead in his hands and lets out a long, shaky breath. "Things have been really, really hard lately." He looks at the ground, and before I know what's happening, he's crying. It's almost a relief. He used to cry all the time, enough that people would tease him, but after the funeral he mostly just…stopped.

I put my arm around his shoulder stiffly, trying not to be as awkward as I feel. He still smells like chlorine from the pool. I feel this weird urge to hug him with both arms. To hold him closer.

A memory springs up of us in the park together last June. Morgan had just fallen out of a tree from the fourth or fifth branch, *scarily* high. I kneeled over him to see if he was breathing, to ask if anything was broken, and he opened his eyes, his huge, dark brown eyes, looked up at me, and maybe I was dizzy from the heat and adrenaline, or maybe it was that his hair was getting long and he was starting to thin out, but he looked like a girl. A really pretty girl.

I shake that thought away.

"I'm sorry, Morgan," I finally mutter towards the floor.

Morgan pulls away and arches his back, taking in a deep breath. For a second, the distance between our bodies feels wrong, but then I don't know why I keep thinking that.

Faggot, I hear my brothers' voices say in my head, and I push it away. "No, I'm sorry for being so off," he says.

"I'm your best friend. I don't care," I say. And it's true, I don't.

Morgan turns towards me, his eyes red from the chlorine or tears, I can't tell. "We're gonna be best friends for ever," he says, his pupils large. "High school, college, jobs…none of that'll get in the way."

As the words come out of his mouth, I wonder if Morgan read my mind, or if maybe I read his. Relief washes over me. We're both worried about the same things. Maybe because we were born on the same day, we have special powers. Like we're cosmic twins, or something. But that's stupid. *Lots* of people were born that day. Lots of people didn't spend three days in the same room during a freak storm though. Who knows?

I nod and offer him another slice of cake. "For ever," I say.

He takes a bite and smiles, his teeth jam-packed with sprinkles. "Good," he says, and I feel a weight shift off my chest as I tell myself that everything is going to be fine. We'll always be Eric and Morgan. Nothing is ever going to change that.

FOURTEENTH BIRTHDAY

MORGAN

It's hot again today, and the air conditioner's still busted. How was there ever a freak snowstorm in September? The idea of a blizzard on a day like today feels impossible.

I wake up early before my alarm, and shuffle into the kitchen, my thigh-length *Creepshow* T-shirt sweat-plastered to my back and armpits, cursing whoever's in charge upstairs for dooming me to life in a place where temperatures crawl up to ninety even in early fall. My long hair sticks to my neck. I pour a bowl of cereal and stare blearily at the linoleum.

"Ugh," Dad says as he emerges from his bedroom, dark spots already forming under his armpits and down his spine. He squeezes into our kitchenette, starts to pour coffee into his work Thermos, then fills it with ice first. He doesn't seem to notice me until he's had his first sip. "You're up early."

"AC's broke," I say.

"You don't say," he says. "Couldn't sleep?"

I spoon bran into my mouth and shake my head.

"Can't blame you," he says. "Coming to the game tonight?"

"Wouldn't miss it for the world," I say. My new high school friend, Jasmine, is dragging me entirely against my will, but I also know my recent game attendance makes Dad happy, and I don't want to let him down.

"That's the spirit," he says. "Happy birthday, by the way. How's fourteen feel?"

Well, I hardly know how to answer that. I can't tell my dad that I don't relate to any boys my age except Eric, and no girls are interested in being friends with me except Jasmine. That the bullying from the guys on *his* football team has only gotten worse, and the only reason I still run every day is because I want to stay fast in case I need to make a quick getaway. Some days, I have my weird feelings under control, but every time I think about getting older in this body, it feels like that Tom Cruise movie where the vampires are in the mine shaft and watching the sunlight get closer inch by inch.

But "Fine" is all I say to Dad. "Pretty much the same, I guess."

"It's a weird time," Dad says. "Next year you get a learner's permit, then a driver's licence at sixteen, then eighteen's the *big* one. Don't get much for fourteen though."

"Acne," I say. I rub a red spot on my jawline that I've been feeling self-conscious about.

Dad laughs. "And maybe these…?" he says. He opens the utility drawer, pulls out a stack of envelopes, and drops them on the counter beside me. A quick glance reveals my name on the top one, but my eyes are still too bleary from sleep to make out much more.

"Grandma's getting senile if she sent this many birthday cards," I say.

"They're not from your grandma," Dad says. His mouth ticks up into a little smile, but then he checks his watch and groans. "I have to get to morning practice. See you tonight."

"Yeah," I say. I give him a perfunctory wave and set my bowl down. The sound of the door closing and his car pulling out of the driveway barely even registers as I focus on the top envelope again, and with a flutter in my chest, Mom's handwriting swims into focus.

The envelope reads, *"Morgan, 14th Birthday."*

I rip it open like there's a golden ticket inside and pull out five sheets of paper – one eight by eleven printer stock and four sheets of higher quality art paper. The top sheet, the white printer paper, has her handwriting on it. I rub my eyes and focus.

Morgan,
Hi, it's Mom.

Sorry there were only two videos, but I'm not looking great these days and I would rather you remember me the way you knew me before this year. I know it's a little vain, but I was pregnant for nine months and labour hurt a lot, so I figure you can humour me. And, also, you can frame these letters or have them scanned into a computer, but I've seen too many VCRs eat tapes to let those be all you have to remember me by. Who even knows if people will still have VCRs by the time you read this? Hard for me to imagine, but then again, I insisted CDs would never replace cassettes.

(Cassettes don't skip when you run with a walkman! Cassettes don't scratch! It's not like I was wrong, everyone else just went insane!)

I'm rambling. Sorry. I actually feel pretty good today, which is getting rarer and rarer, so I can't help getting a little manic. Anyway, happy birthday, my love! I've been thinking a lot about your future, what sort of man you'll grow up to be—

There's a crinkle in the paper and I realize with a jolt of panic that I've clenched my fist. I pause to try and smooth the page back out, but my hands are shaking too much so I quickly give up.

—and, well, since, if you're reading this, I'm not there

56

to see it, I thought I might share some of what I thought up with you... I know people grow and change as they get older or else we'd have a country of nothing but ballerinas and astronauts. I just want you to know how I see you, and how much I love you, and how much faith I have that no matter what you choose to do, you'll do it well.

Love always,
Mom

I set the letter aside, making sure to avoid any wet or greasy spots in our eternally dirty kitchen, and go through the other pages one by one.

Each page is a piece of art – one in watercolour, one in ink, one in charcoal, and one in acrylic paint. The watercolour is a painting of me, muscular and short-haired in an orange Vols jersey, hoisted up by hands rising from the bottom of the page. Sweat plasters hair to my forehead and my face is dirty but I'm smiling, clutching the Heisman Trophy to my chest.

The roof of my mouth feels heavy as I look at the painting. I can hear my pulse in my ears.

I'm smaller in the monochrome ink drawing, only taking up about a quarter of the page, bearded and a little shaggy-haired in a blazer and jeans, standing with my hands in my pockets looking thoughtful in front of a huge blackboard covered in a complicated mathematical formula that looks like something from *Good Will Hunting*.

I feel my face and my lip, where a tiny amount of light brown peach fuzz has already sprouted, imagine growing a beard, and quickly put that page on the bottom of the stack, my throat feeling suddenly dry.

I've got a beard in the charcoal sketch too, but this time with short hair and a white lab coat. There's a stethoscope around my neck, and I'm striding purposefully between a room marked RADIOLOGY and a room marked ONCOLOGY.

Memories of the last days at the hospital flood to the surface. I have to close my eyes and breathe to keep from running to the bathroom to throw up.

I'm beardless in the acrylic painting, thank god, kneeling in profile with a big professional video camera slung over my shoulder, staring intently at whatever I'm filming.

My fingers trace over the pieces of paper, careful not to smudge the charcoal or take flecks off the acrylic, every nerve singing with the thought that she also touched these pages, that every rough bump of paint and ink is a footprint in time. This is the closest I'll ever come to touching her again, and realizing that makes my breath come in short, quivering bursts.

My mother was so talented in so many ways I'm only now learning to recognize – a painter, a gardener, a baker, a deep thinker. But for all her insights, she never knew *me*.

My hands shake so bad I'm afraid I'll damage her art, so I fold it and slip it back in the envelope, then slide it all into the videotape box in the hall closet for good measure.

She never knew the real me and she's gone for ever. She died thinking of me as her son, and unless heaven is real, I will *always* be her son in that last, horrible, infinite moment.

I stay crouched in the hall, sweat and tears coursing down my temples and dripping from my chin. I rub my eyes and pull my knees to my chest, distantly aware of small, desperate chirps escaping my throat, sounding like nothing so much as an animal, wounded, begging for help when it knows none is coming.

Eventually my alarm clock screams, letting me know it's time to wake up for school. Before I can think about what I'm doing, a roar rasps out of my throat and I run to the bedroom, grab the thrift store clock, snatch it from the outlet, and fling it against the wall.

There's a satisfying *crack* and tinkle of glass as guilt, embarrassment, and comforting emptiness rush in to replace the need to cry. I wipe my nose with my forearm and take a breath through clenched teeth. I wash my face with cold water so nobody at the cell block we call a high school will be able to tell I've been crying, throw on a pair of shorts, and head out for another productive, enriching day of ninth grade.

* * *

The field churns below us like fluorescent white noise. I know Eric's jersey number, 32, so I can focus on him running across the grass as the quarterback gets ready to throw the ball. He was never a great choice for the offensive line, and now that he's grown tall and lean, wide receiver suits him way better. Next to me, Jasmine jumps to her feet, clapping and yelling.

Jasmine knows I have complicated feelings about football, but ever since we became friends in Spanish at the beginning of the school year (she called the teacher an illiterate goon in Spanish, the teacher couldn't understand her, I cracked up) she's made it her life's work to pull me out of my shell, even though she's so much cooler than me, with her Cleopatra bangs, red lipstick, and jean jacket covered in band patches. People give her shit, like apparently Latinas aren't supposed to enjoy indie rock or shop at Forever 21, but they're idiots and she's become my best friend. Except for Eric, of course. And to her, apparently leaving my shell means I have to attend the big September game against our rivals the Dogwood Pioneers and cram into the bleachers with the rest of my school and probably most of my town – even if it is my birthday. I'd guess there are close to three thousand people here, all desperate to forget their sons dying overseas for no reason and their daughters wolfing down pills for a momentary escape from their dead end lives.

A spurt of motion catches my attention and I focus on

the field to find Eric as he leaps in the air and catches the pass. He made it onto the junior varsity team just like Dad predicted, and since the varsity wide receiver broke his leg on a quad bike last month, Eric's gotten a lot of time on the field. Carson says Eric has more natural talent in his pinky than Tom Brady. Sometimes I don't even know if Eric *likes* football, but he says it's nice to be good at something and it makes his dad happy. I *try* to tell him he's a good guitarist, try to encourage him by recording him while he plays, but he always gets embarrassed and quits, and half the time he mutters that it's a waste of time since Carson won't pay for his college. It's a football scholarship or a job at the used car lot under his dad's thumb. I know what *I'd* pick too, if those were my choices.

And anyway, while I don't know about the Tom Brady comparison, Eric *is* good. I never would have told him this, but back in junior and youth league I did a lot of covering for him – I was fast enough at snapping off passes that nobody really noticed how often he let tackles through our line. Dad says Eric's found his niche now, and that's definitely part of it – he's never been aggressive enough for close contact play at the line – but if I had to hazard a guess I'd say playing guitar did a lot to get him where he is. A good receiver isn't just fast, he's also good at thinking on his feet and has sensitive, nimble hands.

Jasmine cheers beside me. I look back to Eric and wince. Things aren't going great down on the field, but they aren't hopeless either, and even though we're down by nine points, I can tell Eric hasn't let it get to him. He breaks out of locks with guys half again his size like he's coated in butter, he rolls over defenders' backs and lands on his feet where other guys would crumple to the dirt, and he almost always reads when to push for extra yards and when to dive out of bounds – on the rare occasions he actually gets the ball.

The crowd loves him, *I* love him, and he's the only guy on the field keeping his head in the game, but he's young and small and the quarterback keeps pretending he isn't even there. But then the last play of the third quarter starts, the quarterback fades, and the varsity wide receiver, a junior named something like Colby or Riley, gets hemmed in by four defenders – the Pioneers aren't stupid and they've figured out our QB's clear passing preference. It's too late to try a run, which means the *only* option is a pass to Eric.

My fingers tighten on the bleachers.

The ball flies.

The field rings with the loudest silence I've ever heard.

Eric catches the pass as gracefully as a nurse with a newborn and takes off.

I grit my teeth and distantly become aware that I'm whispering, "*Go, go, go, go!*" One of the Pioneers' safeties breaks off from the older wide receiver, charges towards him, and I yell because I'm certain Eric's about to be flattened, but then he jukes to the side, spins, and he's clear. To the whole stadium's surprise but mine, Eric makes it to the end zone.

Touchdown.

The crowd roars.

This time when Jasmine stands, I'm right beside her, clapping and whooping with everyone else. Our team pulls down the conversion with a *perfect* kick and, as the third quarter draws to a close, we're back in the game.

The band begins blasting out the melody from "Seven Nation Army" and the cheerleaders jump to attention. My chest tightens as my eyes fall on them. They're lit from behind by the sunset, and they're beautiful, of course, because looking and moving beautifully is the whole point of what they do. I'm fixated on their bodies as they move, part admiring, fascinated – and part jealous, I realize. Their tight uniforms fit their bodies perfectly and I couldn't feel more different than them, covered up in my blue hoodie, red T-shirt, faded jeans, and Adidas sneakers stained green from mowing lawns.

Jasmine's hand passes in front of my face. "Like what you see?" she says. She leans back, flips her hair, and rolls her eyes. "Horndog."

I feel a shameful heat rise into my cheeks. I *wish* I was a horndog. I try to make myself feel turned on by the thought of all that flimsy fabric, but nothing happens in that department – which just makes me feel worse. Like something is wrong with me. I think back to our birthday a year ago, to when I almost told Eric my big secret, that I want to be a girl. But since then, I've done everything I can to lock those feelings deep inside of myself, and outside of blow-ups like this morning, I've been…mostly successful. The trick is to stay busy. It's hard to believe I tried to say it out loud just last year.

"Ha, yeah. You caught me," I say.

She winks. "Well, I'm sure they'll all be at Elena's party tonight."

"There's a party at Elena's?"

"Yes," she says. A twinkle appears in her eye. "A *football* party. And you're coming, 'cause Elena's my cousin so we've got an in and 'cause it's your birthday. Don't try coming up with an excuse so you can sit in your room all night listening to that freaky band."

The band she's talking about is Malice Mizer. They're a Japanese goth band from the nineties I found because they dress like girls in half their videos. Not that I would tell anyone that. I swallow and nod.

"Great! We're going!" she says in a voice innocent as birdsong.

Eric's touchdown put the spirit back in the Oak County Wildcats and we come into the fourth quarter strong. The Pioneers screw up the punt return and our defence snatches control back at their thirty yard line. The game continues. The Pioneers drag their feet coming on and off the field, calling a succession of time-outs, clearly trying to run down the clock while they still have a two-point advantage. It's smart, and absolutely not against the rules, but still drives me to hiss and boo with everyone else on our side of the field.

We fight for every inch though, and Eric alone pulls two first downs out of his pocket and squeezes twenty more yards onto his already amazing performance last quarter. Still, despite our fire and renewed spirit, the Wildcats have only managed to push to the thirty yard line when the clock shows four minutes, forty-five seconds.

I know a kick is inevitable, Dad knows a kick is inevitable, and everyone on the field knows a kick is inevitable, but my hands still clench into fists when I watch the Wildcats bunch up tight at the line of scrimmage. Jasmine bounces in her seat. I let out a long breath through my nose. There's the snap, and the ball goes to the holder.

Time moves at half speed. The Wildcats' holder kneels and everyone holds their breath, but then I lean forward and squint – he isn't holding the ball in position for a kick! He's squatting with his back turned to the defence, the ball clutched to his chest. Oh, damn.

The kicker still runs forward, maintaining the illusion that they're attempting a field goal. I look up and finally notice Eric breaking off from the left side of the line, only a single Pioneer bothering to follow him. *Yes.*

But…our team *wouldn't* attempt a trick play with this much on the line. Not when they could *easily* win with a field goal. Right? Dad would never clear it. But then I glance at the sidelines and recognize a look of horror dawning on Dad's face. The kicker mimes kicking, and the Pioneers make like confused dogs, watching where the ball is *supposed* to go, while the holder stands, fades, snaps, and drills the ball straight into Eric's hands.

Eric catches it. Pretty as you please.

He runs. Another touchdown.

The crowd goes insane. I scream myself hoarse.

The clock runs out. Game over.

We won.

Eric won the game.

It was a stupid plan, *so* stupid, but we haven't beaten the Pioneers in fifteen years and folks will probably be talking about this play long after we've graduated.

I watch with a bonfire glow of pride as the older varsity boys pick Eric up and carry him, laughing, off the field. The cheerleaders dance, keeping the magic of the crowd going strong.

"Parking lot's gonna be a crush," Jasmine shouts over the noise. "I'll find us a ride. Meet in front of the cafeteria in fifteen, okay?"

I nod and she wanders off, flitting through the press of students as easy as Eric juked through the Pioneer defence. Eric runs back onto the field, clearly looking for someone

– me? There's a rush in my stomach as I realize the star of the football game is coming to find *me*.

I wave him over and he tracks me down before I can get off the bleachers, and I push through the crowd to get down to the railing. Eric smiles and bounces in place, his eyes glittering with the rush of an insane gamble that worked out.

"You were so good!" I say.

He laughs sheepishly and runs his hand over his sweaty hair and I realize, not for the first time, how much he's grown in the last year. I've been taller for as long as I've known him, but now he's three inches above me at five-nine and a solid hundred and fifty pounds of lean muscle. I'm glad he's kept his long hair, though. It makes us look almost like brothers…or no, wait, that feels gross, but it feels like his shoulder-length curls are his little signal that no matter how much he stays on the jock side of things, he still stands with us weirdos.

"You don't have to pretend you like football," Eric says. "I'm just glad you came."

"No, really!" I say. I wave my arms for emphasis and almost roll myself over the railing. "When you caught that pass? And did the thing? Like *phfwah*? The spin move? So fresh."

"That so, Morgan?" I hear my dad say. I look down to see that he's a few feet away, with a satchel of sports equipment over his shoulder. He adjusts his sunglasses and waves. "Offer's still open if you ever change your mind. I could use a level head to help rein in these hotshots."

I almost laugh, but an insane part of me wants to say yes – if only so I could spend more time with my best friend, or just, like, fill my time with *something*. Junior varsity keeps Eric *way* busier than youth league did, and Jasmine spends every other weekend with her dad, leaving me with not a lot on my plate...

You can only film so many atmospheric shots and mini-documentaries in a town like Thebes, and my DV Handycam tape budget isn't exactly infinite. It's not like I can endlessly watch movies like I want to either. We still have dial-up at the trailer, and the only video rental store within an easy bike ride shut down last February, driven out of business by some internet company that sends DVDs in the mail, which is no use to me since Dad won't use his credit card online. There's still the Blockbuster, but that's four hours, round trip. I've read every book on film history and editing they have at the local library (which wasn't many), along with Stephen King's entire oeuvre, and eventually had to beg the librarian for recommendations. Now I've got a new favourite book in *The Left Hand of Darkness*, but obsessing over a book and spending time with my best friend aren't exactly equivalent.

So, yeah, I think about saying yes, because I'm bored and because I'm lonely.

But also, I would never in a gajillion years actually say yes to playing football again.

"Dad…" I sigh, not able to fully say no to him out loud. I hang my head and let my long hair block out the world, hoping he understands.

"What? You know you were great. Can't blame me for trying…" Dad says. He's in coach-mode now, his tone light and teasing. "Consider it a birthday present to me."

"I'm not sure that's how it works, Dad." I try to laugh it off.

He shrugs and then comes over to shake Eric's hand. "Good job out there, Eric."

"Thanks, Coach Tyler," Eric says.

My dad looks up at me and I watch as he fidgets in place for a moment, clearly trying to think of something to say now that football talk is over. Eventually he just smiles and nods and I return the gesture. I know he cares about me in his own way. It's okay that he has trouble showing it. "All right. Well. See you later, Morgan."

He doesn't say "son", which is something. Maybe he subconsciously picked up on how miserable the word makes me. "Bye," I say and flip my hair out of my eyes. Dad gives me a half smile and walks off towards the gym.

"Anyway," I say, turning back to Eric, "Jasmine's dragging me to a party tonight."

"Elena's, right?" Eric says, his eyes suddenly darting to the end of the field and the lone figure of my dad under the floodlights. "Heard it was supposed to be a consolation prize, but I guess now it's a celebration. I think Nate and some other guys are going."

"Yeah," I say. "You should come. This win was mostly yours, dude. Make it a birthday thing."

"I..." Eric starts. His shoulders sag and he turns back to me. "I don't know. There's an early practice tomorrow, and Coach – Tyler...your dad – wants me to work on some things. I should probably sleep."

"C'mon," I say. "It's our birthday." Eric's eyes focus on the pattern on his helmet and I hear the girlish hitch in my voice, which immediately makes me feel ashamed. "We haven't skipped a birthday since you got chicken pox in third grade..."

He doesn't look up at me, and I can't tell what's suddenly off with him.

"I wish, but I can't," Eric says. He tucks his helmet under one arm and forces a smile as he finally looks up at me on the bleachers above him. "We'll do *something* this weekend, though. I promise."

"Sure," I say. "I get it." I slide down until my arms are hooked over the railing.

The rest of the team finally realizes that Eric has drifted away from them.

"Eric! MVP!" one of the guys shouts.

"Eric! Yo, Eric!"

"Wi-ld-cats. Wi-ld-cats," another cheers.

They rush around him, shielding him behind a wall of muscular bodies. Eric smiles sheepishly and lets himself drift away from me and back onto the field, our conversation clearly over. I let him go without trying to say goodbye.

As they pull him away from me, Nate and Chud, a grade above us and way ahead in growth spurts, catch my eye and sneer. Nate blows me a kiss and Chud makes a jerking off motion. I toss up a double bird and there's a moment where none of us move. They check to see if Eric's looking and I check to see if Dad's looking, and sadly for me, it's a no on both counts. *Oh, fuck.*

The coast clear, Nate and Chud charge for the stairs, pushing past people filing out for the parking lot. I run. My daily workouts pay off. Racing in the opposite direction, I jump from the fifth bleacher, land with a roll in the grass, and disappear behind the bathrooms, praying I've lost them.

"Keep running, faggot!" I hear Chud yell.

"Fuck you, meathead," I swear under my breath.

I sigh heavily and feel my heart rate slow. The cold cinder block walls of the bathroom chill the back of my neck as I let my head roll. After a few minutes, I peek around the corner and watch as Eric is guided away to chants and slaps on his shoulder. He never turns around, never looks back.

ERIC

"Waffle House?" Mom asks as we pull up to the restaurant. She gives Dad a tired look. "Really?"

"It's a Wildcats tradition!" Dad says. "Whenever you beat the Pioneers, you get Waffle House. Right, Eric?"

I shrug. The *rest* of the team's getting pizza right now, but what can I do? It was embarrassing enough having Dad drag me away – no reason to also get yelled at. "Last time we beat them was a year before I was born. I wouldn't know."

"But *this* Waffle House, Carson?" It's not good news when Mom uses Dad's name instead of "honey" or "sug".

I crane my neck to look through the windshield and my good mood, already strained from the car ride, evaporates at the sight of Peyton looking tired and sweaty behind the counter, shuffling back and forth between a grill and a waffle iron.

I still remember when he got this job a week after he turned sixteen, the screaming match he had with Dad over not taking a part-time job at the dealership, how Peyton yelled that he shouldn't need a job at all with how well-off we are, but if he had to have one, he'd rather slam his dick in a car door than work for Dad at the dealership. I can still hear the sound of thick footsteps, followed by a hard thud, the sound of a body hitting the floor, Peyton's heavy breathing.

"Nobody gave me anything," Dad had said. "Nobody made you blow your knee out. Now, son, the job offer at the dealership was a *favour* to your dumb ass, and you just threw it in my face like an ingrate. This is what happens when you're ungrateful. Don't ever ask me for anything again."

"I won't," I heard Peyton yell back.

Peyton's been working at Waffle House ever since. This Waffle House, to be specific.

"They're brothers," Dad says as he turns off the car – this year's newest model. He waves Mom's concerns away like a cloud of mites as he steps out of the car, and we, his dutiful servants, shuffle behind. Mom gives me a look that could be pity or an apology. I shrug.

"I'm sure Peyton wants to congratulate him and wish him a happy birthday," Dad says as he opens the restaurant door. He doesn't hold it open for Mom and it closes in her face. I hold back a growl and open the door for Mom.

She smiles weakly as she walks through.

"I'm sure you're right," Mom says, but her voice is flat and Dad isn't even listening.

Peyton notices us as soon as we enter. He turns to say something to the old woman running the register, his eyes twitch for a moment, and he scowls, but otherwise he doesn't acknowledge us.

Dad sidles into a booth against the divider near the grill and we follow him, me and Mom on one side while Dad takes up the entire seat on the other. Nobody says anything for a while. Mom checks her lipstick in the faint reflection of the laminated menu. I roll my neck, trying to work out a sore spot. Dad drums his fingers on the table. Eventually the old woman approaches us with a smile and a voice like a million packs of cigarettes.

"Evenin', folks! Know what you want yet, or should we start with dr—"

"Him," Dad says. Me and Mom look up to find him smiling pleasantly, his thick finger pointed at Peyton. My brother doesn't turn but I see his shoulders stiffen as he stops what he's doing at the grill. Meat sizzles. Dolly Parton warbles from the jukebox. "We want him as our server."

"Little Peyton?" Her smile widens, but it doesn't reach her eyes. "I'm real sorry but he's on grill tonight. I'll be happy to—"

"I will tip you twenty-five dollars," Dad says, slowly

and evenly, "if you ignore our table and watch the grill for a minute so that boy can serve us."

"I…" She closes one eye and chews her pen. Dad sniffs loudly. Before the woman can make a decision, though, Peyton's hand appears on her shoulder.

"It's one table, Dee," he says. "Slow night. I can handle both. You go take a smoke break."

"You sure?"

He nods. She smiles and backs towards the door, pointedly not looking at Dad. "Okay, well, just holler if you need anything! Such a nice young man we have here."

I've heard Peyton called a lot of things, but never a "nice young man". Then again, looking up at him now, with the sheen of sweat on his forehead and neck, and the aura of fatigue around his eyes, he looks more like a tired, disciplined adult than the borderline bully I've grown up with.

"Dad," Peyton says. "Mom. Eric. What's up?"

"Didn't you hear?" Dad says.

"I've been here all night," Peyton says.

"We beat the Pioneers!"

"Oh," Peyton says. He yawns into his elbow and pulls a notepad from his belt, blinking slowly. "Hell yeah."

"Shouldn't you congratulate your brother?" Dad says.

"Carson…" Mom says, but Dad snaps a stony glare at her.

"Congrats, I guess," Peyton says.

75

"Th-thanks," I say, hating feeling like we're all pawns in one of Dad's games.

"Plus it's your birthday. Damn."

I nod.

"Well then. Think of something weird to put in a waffle and I'll make it for you."

I've never known him to be this thoughtful, and I'm not sure what to say, so I just smile and nod.

"Know what y'all want to drink?"

"Water," I say.

"Decaf," Dad says.

"Orange juice," Mom says. Her eyes dart to Dad's. "Only fill the glass about two-thirds of the way full, please." She fiddles in her purse and I catch a glimpse of a small bottle of vodka rattling between her wallet and house keys.

"Jenny..." Dad says.

"Carson," she says. She lifts her chin as if daring him to say something else. A moment of electric potential passes between them, but Dad seems to blink.

"Coming right up." Peyton excuses himself to check the grill and fill our drinks.

"So, Eric," Dad says. He leans forward and laces his fingers together, his near-fight with Mom already forgotten. "You did good tonight. Real good. But here's where I think you could stand to improve..."

He keeps talking. He's always talking, and we're always

76

listening. I stare over his shoulder and let my eyes unfocus, nodding and saying "uh-huh" just enough that he'll believe I'm still conscious.

Peyton brings our food, and we dig in, just barely pretending that we're a family.

My bedsheets tangle under me. Sleep won't come. Every time I close my eyes, I remember Morgan's face as he looked down on me from the bleachers after the game, his long brown hair blowing in the breeze, his eyes bright with expectation, then suddenly dimming when I told him I couldn't go to Elena's party. He was right, of course: we've only spent one birthday apart since we were born, and then only because of chicken pox. We were so mad that our parents had kept us separate that we took a week-long vow of silence.

No one really knows this, but I only tried out for junior varsity, *really*, because I wanted to spend more time on the bench. In youth league I was good enough – even without Morgan to make me look better – that I got put into every single game and I was sick of that. But as a junior varsity player, I hoped that all I'd be doing is working out with friends a few times a week, doing homework by a football field every Friday night, and secretly practising guitar chords against my helmet.

I imagined it would be way less stressful, but then Terry

Mack got injured and ruined my carefully laid plans, like an asshole, and I'm stuck playing wide receiver every week instead of daydreaming on the bench. On top of that, I have to practise extra to catch up with the rest of the guys. I wasn't lying to Morgan when I said that Coach Tyler had me doing stuff tomorrow. Coach would be so pissed at me if I showed up tired and worn out.

From my bed, I reach out in the dark, hook my finger around the second smallest string on my guitar, and pluck a series of B notes.

Football gets Dad and Isaac off my back, and I can tell it makes Morgan's dad happy too. After Morgan stopped playing, everyone just waited for him to come back; sometimes I feel like I'm doing this for both of us.

Both of us.

At least Morgan came tonight. He seemed better than usual, which is a relief. With my miserable practice schedule, we've gotten to hang out so rarely, and more and more I feel that pressure at the back of my neck that means Morgan needs me. Jasmine's nice, and I consider her a friend or at least an acquaintance, but has she known Morgan for fourteen years? No. Has she stood by him through everything from scraped knees to a dead parent? No. Does she just *know* when he's sad? No way.

I sigh, roll over, and watch through my window as a van trundles by in the orange glow of street lights.

Maybe it's not normal to think about Morgan this

much. My mind races back to a sleepover we had a few weeks ago – he'd just gotten out of the shower before bed, and I'd barged into my bedroom without knowing he was still getting dressed. He was standing with his back to me and I froze.

I see other boys' bare backs constantly in the locker room, but his was so slender, and so smooth, with hips that flared out just a little, and with his long brown hair plastered all the way between his shoulder blades…for a moment, just a *moment*, my brain screamed that I'd walked in on a half-naked girl and I slammed the door behind me.

Who knows what the hell I should think about that. It's probably just my head being weird and crossing wires because I worry about him so much. My cell phone chirps and I flip it open with a groan – one text from Isaac and one from Morgan. Not sure how I missed the first one. I open the message from Isaac first.

Happy birthday lil bro! Heard you whipped Dogwood ass tonight! Four years in a row I lost to those assholes, and now here you are in 9th grade. Respect! You've probably got people telling you to not let it go to your head. Fuck that. You'll never be 14 again so go do something crazy.

Staying in on a Friday night after a big win suddenly feels even more pathetic. Count on Isaac to make me feel like a baby even when he's not here.

I open the text from Morgan and have to cover my

mouth to keep from laughing out loud. He's sent a picture with him and Jasmine in the foreground, their faces sombre like the couple in *American Gothic*, while in the background a pixellated girl is tumbling down from a kegstand, her panicked face blurred as foam sprays everywhere. The text below it reads, *Wish you were here!*

That settles it.

I roll out of bed, grab my glasses, slip into jeans and a Dinosaur Jr T-shirt, cram my Razr into my pocket, tie my hair back, *consider* grabbing my guitar, but decide I don't want to be "that guy", and slip down the hall past my parents' room – it is *technically* after my Friday night curfew, which is going to make this tricky. I pass Isaac's old room, then knock on Peyton's door as lightly as I can.

"Peyton," I hiss. He doesn't answer after the first light knock so I tap his bedroom door a little harder, keeping an ear out for any signal that Mom or Dad are onto me. "*Peyton!*"

"*What?*" He yanks the door open with a look of surprise. We stand eye to eye. He's still not used to me being the same height and weighing almost as much as him. He smells like sausage and flour. "What are you doing? I thought you had practice in the morning."

"I'm skipping it," I whisper. Peyton actually looks impressed – he used to go out more, or I feel like I remember that, but between working twenty hours a week and actually paying attention in his junior year (nobody gives you a pass when you're not on the team), he's tired all the time. "Now I need your help." He braces his elbow on the door frame and motions for me to continue. "I know you like to mess with me, but we're in brother-code territory here, and if you don't come through for me now—"

"Jesus *Christ*, why do you have to be so dramatic all the time? Get to the point."

"I need to borrow your car." Normally I would never ask Peyton for something this crazy, especially after what happened tonight at Waffle House. But really, it's *our* car. It was Isaac's before he left for college, and it's Peyton's now, and when he turns eighteen and moves out, it will be mine. So really, I'm just borrowing against my own future property.

"Fuck no," Peyton says, leaning back like I'm a bad smell. "You're fourteen, idiot."

"Then give me a ride," I say.

"You know Dad'll kill both of us, right?"

"Call it a birthday present!" I say, desperation creeping into my voice.

He rubs his face and sighs. "Gimme some details," he says.

I square my shoulders and raise my chin. "It's that girl, Elena. I'm sure you've seen her – junior? Short? Curvy? It's *her* post-game party. And I know her cousin."

Peyton raises his eyebrows and tugs at his lip, suddenly intrigued.

"You're not talking about that Mexican your little gay friend always hangs out with?" he says.

I want to punch him in the neck, or at least yell that Jasmine's from Dalton, and Morgan's straight, but I have to pick my battles, so I frown and nod. "You're not trying to get with her, are you? She's *clearly* after the gaylord. Brother to brother? That's not a good love triangle to step into."

"Whatever," I say. "It's not like that. There'll be *more* girls there. Cheerleaders."

Peyton takes a long, deep breath, then shrugs and sighs. "Fine," he says. "But you *better* at least touch a tit or something."

I cringe inwardly, but try not to show it. "Yup, definitely the plan."

After a little tactical espionage action (mostly me almost breaking my neck trying to climb off the roof while Peyton stares at his phone – the speed with which he managed the shimmy down with a never-fully-recovered ligament is a testament to how often he must *still* sneak out), we're on the road, headed for the other side of town, deep-night blue and flickering street-light orange bathing the community theatre that marks the centre of downtown while Young Jeezy's "Soul Survivor" blasts through our open windows, shattering the otherwise perfect small-town silence.

I bob my head to the beat and drum on his car door,

trying to make Peyton think I'm cool enough to be worth all this effort.

"I'm sorry, by the way," I say, raising my voice to be heard over the wind and the radio.

"Eh?" he says. He turns down the volume and glances at me.

"For tonight," I say. "At your work. It wasn't my idea to come. I'm sorry Dad—"

"Don't apologize for the shit he does," Peyton says. His hands squeeze the steering wheel, the fake leather creaking.

"I know, but—"

"Some advice?" he says. "Brother to brother? Stop trying to impress him. Stop trying to please him. Unless you're a golden boy like Isaac, you won't like what it costs you. *Everybody* can't be team captain. *Everybody* can't be recruited for a full ride at the University of Tennessee. There aren't enough captain positions and scholarships in the world, and you're just fucking yourself if you try to compete in a world with guys like Isaac in it. Dad 's an asshole for making us do that. Among other things."

"I…I know he can be a jerk, but he didn't mess up your knee." I want to add, *You stopped trying to impress him and look what it's got you*, but I don't.

"No?" Peyton says. "I guess all he did was scream at me every night for not making first string and push me to lift weights I couldn't handle. Fuck me for being a fourteen-year-old who listened when Dad told me I had to choose

83

between more squats and getting to eat that weekend, right? Fuck me for not pushing things when my knee blew out and he told me to *walk it off.*"

I always wondered why his injury was as bad as it was, why it never seemed to heal completely. He probably should have had surgery.

"I didn't know," I say. My eyes fall on the dashboard and it takes all my effort not to look at his leg and the brace he still wears over his pants sometimes.

"Better for him if I just looked stupid." Peyton runs his hand through his hair and twists his mouth. "I know we don't get along. I know I'm an asshole. Just…listen to me on this one thing, okay? Don't let him eat you alive."

"Okay," I say. "I'll think about it."

"Damn right," he says. "And tell the homo I said congratulations for getting out while the getting was good."

I'm not sure what to say after that, so I don't say anything, just sit with my hands in my lap, wondering what else I don't know about my family and hating what I *do* know.

Neat sidewalks and wooden fences give way to rusted, warped chain-link and concrete riddled with grass-choked cracks. Pristine storefronts give way to strip malls and fluorescent buzzing convenience stores. Mateo's Tiendita is dark and empty, has been since he fell on his hip and moved in with his oldest son last spring. They say they have plans to reopen it once he gets better, but I haven't seen him in months. Hungry-looking dogs of no discernible breed sit, eyes distant, in yards with almost no greenery. More and more trailer parks replace foreclosed houses every day, sprouting up like kudzu. When did it get so hard to find this place beautiful?

Eventually we pull onto a street I don't recognize and roll up to a ranch-style house crammed with cars, and I realize I never gave Peyton directions, just told him it was at Elena's house.

"How'd you know—"

"I *used* to get invited to parties," he says. I don't have to ask why the football team wouldn't want him around now. Tonight's favour and weird brotherly talk aside, he's been a sour, confrontational asshole since the injury. And, as much as I hate to admit it, I can see how no young athlete with the world in front of them wants a limping, scowling reminder of what they could lose hanging around.

Elena's sprawling yard is surrounded by a dogwood forest on three sides. Rihanna blasts from the house, drowning out even Peyton's stereo. Kids are sprawled all over the yard and filter in and out the front door, disappearing with empty hands and reappearing with Solo cups.

Peyton gives me a wolfish grin. "Enjoy it while you can, bud."

I swallow a lump in my throat and adjust my hair –

this is way more of a real party than I expected and part of me feels slightly nervous about what I've just gotten myself into.

"Thanks, man," I say, hiding any fears I might have. "Really." I hold out my fist. He bumps it, we do the explosion, and with that I'm free. I jump out of the car and Peyton tears away, back down the gravel road.

I decide to search for Morgan inside first, and when I open the front door about fifteen kids turn and stare at me. I start to back away, but then they smile and cheer when they recognize me. This party is for me, sort of, and I know I should feel like royalty here instead of a little kid who snuck out past their bedtime.

I clear my throat. "Anybody seen Morgan or Jasmine?" I ask. Some of them shrug and the rest go back to what they were doing. "Morgan's a freshman? Long hair? About this tall?" More shrugging. *Why* is Morgan so good at keeping his head down? "Jasmine? Wears lipstick all the time? She's Elena's cousin?"

"Did somebody say my name?" Elena pokes her head out from the kitchen, her waist-length black hair swaying. She gives me a curious look, her pretty red lips pursed, and my mouth goes dry.

"I'm looking for Morgan and Jasmine?" I say, trying to stand up a little straighter and look a little cooler. She squints like she's trying to remember something.

"They were here earlier, I think…one second." She

yells something out the back window and eventually a male voice calls back. "Jasmine's ride hasn't left yet, and I guess the little dude rode his bike and it's still chained up behind the garage. I think I saw them headed for the backyard a while ago. Good luck!"

She smiles and I wave awkwardly before I circle around to the back of the house where a bonfire looms in the centre of the yard.

"Hey, Potter!" a familiar voice calls. I look up to find some other varsity and junior varsity guys around the bonfire, specifically Nate and Chud. They seem happy to see me tonight, but I guess I did win them the game. Nate's a sophomore and always has his arm around a cheerleader. If my life were a high school movie he would be typecast as the rich asshole whose dad wants to shut down the community centre, but we're nobodies in a shitty Appalachian town, so he lives in a trailer in the same park as Morgan. Chud's a little shorter than Nate, but built like a brick, just pounds and pounds of muscle under a layer of fat, with a head like a rock that's covered in acne.

They call me "Potter" because I brought *Deathly Hallows* to my first junior varsity practice and it fell out of my backpack, so now despite whatever else I accomplish, I'm the dipshit nerd who reads books about wizards.

"Catch!"

"What?" I just barely notice a can flying for my head and catch it without thinking, then realize it's a beer. Am

I supposed to open it right now? Do I just stand here and chug it? I haven't tried beer again since last year on my birthday with Isaac. "Uh. Thanks."

"Come sit," Nate says. I pause, Morgan on my mind, but then my gaze drifts to his side where Susan, a freshman cheerleader, is sitting next to him. I stare at her heart-shaped face and spray of freckles in the bonfire light. She smiles and does a little wave and my stomach lurches. I should keep looking for Morgan, but I've never gotten to hang out with the cheerleaders before...

I find an empty space on one of the logs next to the quarterback, a red-haired junior named Jason. He claps me on the shoulder and taps my beer with his. I crack mine open and taste it, and it's way more bitter tasting than the Corona. I don't want to finish it, but I also want to look cool, so I keep sipping at it while the guys talk about the game. They tell me they've never seen a freshman play like I did tonight. Where was I hiding those moves all season?

"The bench, mostly," I say. They slap their knees and cackle, but I didn't think it was very funny.

"If you keep it up, we might make state next year," says Chud.

"That's, uh," I say. "That's a lot of pressure."

"Pressure, huh?" Jason says. He rubs his chin and smiles. "Maybe *you've* forgotten the last fifteen seconds of the game, but *I* haven't." I take a long sip of beer and shrug.

Jason jabs a finger at me and I blink. "That play was inspired. You act like a chill dude, with your surfer haircut and that slow way you talk, like all you want to do is hang out and listen to music and strum that guitar I see you with. But there's a part of you that *loves* chaos and conflict. You, young Eric, will *never* be a man satisfied with the easy way."

"Y...yeah?"

"Yeah!" Jason says. "I doubt you'll be happy without it."

"He's drunk," Susan says. She leans over to whisper, her bare arm brushing mine, and I blush more than the heat from the bonfire can account for.

"*In vino veritas,*" Jason says. An empty can flies by his head and he laughs.

"Nobody knows what that *means*, you fucking nerd!" Nate yells.

Jason keeps talking and I let his praise wash over me. Together with the alcohol, which is working way faster than I thought it would, Morgan slips from my mind. The fire warms my face, and I smile as Susan hands me another beer.

MORGAN

"Ow!"

"Sorry!" I say.

Jasmine and I stumble forward a few steps, and I look back to see a guy and a girl mostly in silhouette against the distant orange glow of the bonfire, their clothes rumpled and their shadowed faces angry at the interruption. "Sorry. I couldn't see you."

"Come on, man," the guy whispers and I think I recognize him from algebra.

The sound system starts blasting Justin Timberlake as Jasmine grabs my hand and leads me further into the woods. Barely any light from the bonfire bleeds through the trees, just enough for me to see Jasmine's outline and hints of her colourful outfit as she nestles between two oak trees and pats for me to sit down next to her. The beginnings of the fall's leaves crunch under my feet as I fold my legs beneath me. The air is still liquid in the heatwave.

"How'd you know about this spot?" I say. I lean back into the tree and let out a long breath. "It's, uh, pretty far out here."

"Me and Elena explored all through these woods when we were little," she says. I hear her rummaging in her purse. "No cable, so all there was to do out here was sword fight with sticks and push over dead trees."

"Why would you push over dead trees?" I say. "Where's the fun in that?"

"It made a lot of noise." She laughs. "There's some choice woods on the south edge of your trailer park so I *know* you and Eric must have done it too."

"We never thought of it," I say. I pull my knees to my chest and fiddle with the tears in my jeans. "Plus, we didn't move there until after Mom died."

"Oh god, I'm sorry," Jasmine says. "I forgot…I didn't mean to bring it up. Are you okay?"

I rub my forehead and shake my hair out, surprised by how quickly a bad feeling slides off my brain after two beers. Maybe I should drink more often.

"It's fine. I mean it hurts but it's fine."

Things get quiet for a while, which I'm okay with. I know Jasmine's trying to be respectful, giving me distance to process my feelings. It's not how Eric would do it, though – Eric always works out these comedy bits for when I start to feel sad. He'll make me laugh so hard my stomach hurts.

His most recent series of bad jokes involves nonchalantly stating horrible opinions about my favourite movies over and over until I crack. "I started *Pan's Labyrinth* the other day, but who wants to *read* a movie? Next I tried *Princess Mononoke*, but would you believe it was a cartoon? As if I've got any interest in *cartoons*. And don't even get me started on *The Crow*! There's just no point including violence and foul language like that!" Inevitably I'll get worked up, he'll laugh, and I won't be able to help but laugh with him. Just thinking about what his next bad movie take might be makes me smile.

In the silence Jasmine riffles through her purse until she finds whatever she's looking for. The wind starts to blow, parting the canopy and letting moonlight filter through, and I watch in the silver light as she parts her lips, eyes half lidded, and reapplies her lip gloss. Everything about it – her lips, the arch of her back, the way her thigh slips out from under her skirt – holds me in place. It makes me feel like some hidden, private world is being opened before me.

But then she sees me looking and I feel like a deer in headlights. My face flushes, ashamed, but then Jasmine smiles and I realize Jasmine wants to be seen. For a moment, I let my mind wander and I think maybe there are ways of living where I might *want* someone to look at me like I'm looking at Jasmine right now too.

She sidles close, drapes her legs over my lap, and touches my shoulder. What is she doing? Why is there a look on her face like she's figured out a secret? We've never touched like this before and I can feel my shoulders tense, my hands searching for balance in the dried-up leaves as she shifts her body weight onto mine.

"Don't look so scared, Morgan." She laughs, leaning closer.

My heart races, and I can't tell if this is the desire I'm *supposed* to have felt this whole time, or if I just want to run. Didn't realize that desire could feel like panic. Her hips shift against me and her fingers come up to brush a long strand of hair out of my face. I swallow painfully, my mouth dry.

"I saw you watching me," she says. "Do you think I'm pretty?" I can smell beer on her breath, but more than that, I smell her mango shampoo, a hint of strawberry from her lip gloss...

I nod. Jasmine lets her hand rest against my shoulder and brushes my neck with her long fingers. She leans in, lips parting, breath coming slow and deep – or is that mine? Who can say? Something touches my fingers and at first I flinch, thinking it's a bug, but then I glance down and see her other hand on mine, feel her fingers lace into mine. Her lips press against my lips, and suddenly I'm having my first kiss.

At first it feels like nothing, but then I find myself

fantasizing that I'm Jasmine, that I'm the one being watched, the one radiating beautiful smells and glowing in the moonlight, and suddenly I feel what I think I've been *meant* to feel this whole time. I lean into her and rest my hands on her hips. She guides my hands under her shirt, where they graze up to her ribcage. Her skin is so soft and I imagine it's my own skin and I'm kissing a boy. I imagine him running his fingers through my hair, and how small I would feel in his arms, and how soft my chest and thighs would be against him. I imagine his hand at the base of my spine, running up my side, cupping my chin, squeezing my thigh. I imagine a *lot* of things.

But then the fantasy keeps going.

And then the boy is *me* – taller every day, with gawky shoulders, and the shadow of a moustache on his upper lip.

I pull back, keeping my eyes clenched shut.

"What's wrong?" Jasmine says.

I shake my head.

"Did I do something wrong?" Her voice sounds like broken Christmas ornaments.

"No," I say. I can hear my own voice shaking. I force a smile but can't open my eyes. "No, this is…this is great. I love this. But it's getting late. And. Uh." My brain thrums like a generator as it searches for an excuse. "And Eric might still be awake, so I should try stopping by to say hello while it's still our birthday."

Jasmine stares at me for a long time. I feel like I might sink into the forest around us, just disappear. But then she smiles and slaps her forehead.

"That's just my luck," she says softly. I wonder what she's talking about, but then a laugh escapes her throat.

"What is?"

She looks at me with the sincerest amusement, shakes her head, and sighs.

"Of *course* the first boy I ever kiss is gay."

I start to protest, but then she pulls me in for a hug, so I hug her back and consider if she's right. Could I be gay? Could all these weird, painful feelings I've had over the past…whole life be solved like that? *Gay.* I mean, it's not like the idea hasn't occurred to me before, but it's different hearing it from someone else. I've even looked at gay porn once, when Dad wasn't home, but the video I found of two muscular dudes growling and pounding each other made me feel kind of wrong and unwelcome.

It just doesn't feel quite right, like a shirt put on backwards or a radio tuned to a grainy station. Thinking of guys has never given me a…turned me on. I mean, I've only ever touched myself on four occasions, and honestly it was just…strange. Not good strange. It just means I have to think about that whole aspect of my anatomy, which twists my stomach. But I could never say any of that to Jasmine, so I just shrug. "I don't think I am. I don't know…"

"That's okay," Jasmine says. "My aunt Sofia said it took her some time to figure it out." She pulls back and I release the breath that was caught in my chest.

"Okay, well, I should really get going – I don't want to miss Eric, so—" I move to get up.

"Be honest," she says with a smile. "You like Eric, right? Or, I mean, are you like *with* Eric? Like a secret forbidden love thing? You can tell me."

"What! No, I—"

But my mind flashes. Eric with his shirt off at the pool. Eric walking in on me in nothing but a towel. Eric hovering over me that time I fell from the tree. Eric smiling up at me after the game, his face boyish and handsome, even with the dirt all over it. Eric's body, strong and warm, next to mine in bed, more difficult to ignore at each sleepover. These thoughts and more rush up, causing all my speech neurons to misfire. I tell myself that it's only Eric, only because we're so close.

"I won't tell anybody," she whispers. "I promise."

Jasmine watches me carefully. She's wrong, because she *has* to be wrong, but…I don't know what to really say, how to tell her the truth of what I really feel.

"I'm not sure." I sigh, realizing I'm not going to win this battle. "Just…can we not talk about this any more?" I stand on shaking legs and swat dead leaves from my jeans.

"Okay," she says. She squeezes my hand and we start to

walk back to the house. Jasmine must sense how tense I still am because she bumps my hip with her own.

We step into the clearing and the first thing I see, like the universe is either mocking me, doing me a favour, or both, is Eric.

Eric is here.

Eric, who's not even supposed to be at this party. He has one foot up on a log, like some kind of conqueror, with his curly blond hair chaotically erupting from the bun he keeps it in. I watch in shock as he chugs from a can, chin high, while a group of jocks and cheerleaders chant their support.

"Well, well, well," Jasmine says. She pokes me in the ribs. "Look who it is."

I rub my forehead, but can't help smiling.

Jasmine's hand escapes from mine. "You should go over there." She gives me a tiny, sideways grin then takes off, back towards the house. As if. There's no way I'm going over there. The only things stopping those idiots from grinding my head into the dirt are the fact that my dad's their coach and the abundance of witnesses. I sigh and start to shuffle past the bonfire, my head down. Jasmine shoots me a thumbs-up and winks.

"Morgan!" Eric calls out. I freeze and look up to see him spike the now-empty can on the ground and barrel across the yard towards me. I don't know whether to dodge or meet him in the middle so I just laugh nervously and hold my arms out wide. He collides with me like an especially gentle freight train, wrapping his arms under my armpits and lifting me, swinging me around like a rag doll.

"Happy birthday!" he says.

I can't help but laugh at first, but then the strength of his arms registers, and the faint smell of sweat on him, and I notice how my legs are kicking, how my laugh is a little too delighted, how I'm blushing and my neck tingles, and …and…

Fuck.

Maybe Jasmine is right.

Maybe I *am* gay?

Eric loses his balance and falls back, landing with a breathless gasp and me on top of him. I brace myself on his chest to see if he's all right, and his breath comes back with a laugh as my hair falls around our faces, blocking out the whole world. I feel his leg move against mine and realize we're tangled together, and the more I try not to think of it the more I do. I pull my hair behind my ear and something in that gesture gets his attention. Our gazes lock and I can't *not* notice how fast his heart is beating against my palm.

"Gay!" somebody yells from across the yard. I don't even know if they're yelling about me, about *us*, but my face turns hot and I shoot to my feet.

"Here, man," I say, offering a hand to help Eric up.

He struggles to stand. How much has he had to drink?

"Wow, yeah, okay," Eric says as he wobbles forwards.

"Come on, birthday boy," I say kindly. I lead him towards the house by the shoulder. I will myself not to notice how firm and strong his shoulder feels under my fingers, how his muscles coil and shift as we walk through the door. "We should get you home," I manage.

"Sure, sure," Eric says, following me like a kitten.

We walk past the group of kids hanging out in the living room. They barely look at me, but wave goodbye to Eric. He gives them a sloppy grin in return.

Once out the front door, we make our way to where I left my bike. I'm suddenly weirdly grateful that I was so late getting to the parking lot that Jasmine had lost our ride. I ended up riding my bike here, while Jasmine caught a lift with someone else.

"Sleepover!" Eric says. "Let's watch *The Crow* again!"

"Are you joking?" I say. "You hate that movie."

"Yeah, but *you* love it, and I love *you*, dude."

Dude. Dude feels…wrong, like a put-off, but Eric's smile says otherwise. I can't help but give him a goofy grin in return, enjoying this looser, even sillier side of my best friend. I'm coiling the bike chain around my forearm when, out of the blue, Eric reaches out, eyes serious, and strokes his fingers through my hair. I feel a wave of heat crawl up my neck and down from my cheeks. Horror mingles with the pleasure – because of the possibility of someone seeing, because of what this could mean, because of some other disaster I haven't thought of. But also, it does definitely feel pretty good.

"Uh... ?" I manage to say.

"Leaves," Eric says. He steps back and sways a little. I reach out to steady him, only to grab his chest, feel how hard it is, and turn even redder. "You had leaves in your hair."

"Oh," I say.

There's only one way to undo this weirdness. I notice a brown spot on his cheek from when he fell, lick my finger, and rub it off. He lets out this rough little laugh, more grown-up and deep than it has any right to be, and leans into my hand. "You had a...a smudge..."

"Thanks," he says. He takes my hand between both of his and looks suddenly serious. "You're *such* a good friend, dude. Like, *what*? It's crazy! Have I told you I love you lately?"

He's drunk. He's so drunk. I need to get him home.

"You *just* said it," I say, and my face has to be glowing at this point. "But before that? Not since we were little. Our dads made us stop in second grade, remember?"

"Well!" Eric says with a stamp of his foot. "You're my best friend and I love you!"

"I love you too," I mutter.

I put a leg over my bike and I turn around to look at

him and notice his glasses are missing. "Where are your glasses?" I ask.

Eric touches his face and shrugs. I start to worry, which is almost a relief since it's something to focus on besides being flustered, but then I remember his family's loaded and he has a million pairs of glasses at home.

"Okay, well, come on then." I position myself to stand on the pedals and pat the seat behind me. He wraps his arms around my chest, and I *hate* it – I *hate* that Jasmine was even a little right, but my body responds to his closeness. I'm just confused, I tell myself. I'm fourteen, I'm a nervous wreck, I'm hormonal, and my body doesn't know what to do with something like this except…well. It's Jasmine's fault, really – she planted the idea in my head and my idiot brain's running wild with it. Feeling Eric's chest and stomach against my back makes me feel so small, and I'll be damned if that isn't an addictive idea, being small with someone you trust. Maybe…I mean we sleep in the same bed. Would he think it was weird if I wiggled my back against him one night? Would he wrap himself around me in his sleep? It wouldn't have to be anything but that. Friends can cuddle, right? But then Eric lets out a sigh and his breath washes warm down my neck and I shiver.

Would it be bad if it were more? I shake my head – I'm not precisely sober either. Best to hit the road for now and think about this stuff with a clear head.

"Let me know if you need to puke," I say to Eric as I start pedalling. He howls at the moon as we pull through the driveway and out onto the street.

I laugh as the wind whips my hair and we howl together.

ERIC

Street lights and a buzzing Krispy Kreme sign slither and twist into glowing serpents. Did I lose my glasses? I remember Susan borrowing them and asking if she looked cute, and me telling her yes because I thought I was supposed to, even though I couldn't see. I crane my head back and breathe in, smelling old rubber, dried leaves, a distant barbecue. And here, Morgan. Morgan, who just smells like *Morgan*. In front of me. In my arms. My best friend. I bury my face in the crook of his neck and laugh at nothing in particular, at how funny the world can be, at how weird it is that he's a boy.

How weird it is that he's a boy.

I wonder if that's occurred to him. I try to focus on the thought, to pull it apart and examine it, but my brain feels as numb as my nose and the tips of my fingers. Still, it *feels* like a revelation.

Who knew beer was so good? I crane my head up and take a deep, bracing breath. The smear of the heavens twirls as Morgan's bike takes a turn and my breath hiccups as I realize how big everything is, and how small we are, and how in the whole span from the first star, to the end of everything, this moment will never be seen again. This thought makes me dizzy, so I wrap my arms tighter around Morgan's chest and press my face into the back of his neck, into his brown hair.

"So I read something crazy about *The Crow*," Morgan says. It's been his favourite movie since we found an old VHS copy at the McKay's in Knoxville. He fell in love with it immediately. Usually I tease him about it, but I just want to hear him talk.

"Tell me," I say.

"So Eric Draven—"

"Who?" I say.

"The *main character*!" he says. "God, dude, we've watched it three times."

"I never paid *attention*," I say. "It was an excuse to spend time with you."

He's quiet for half a street, and I feel his body shift under my hands. I lean to look at his face, but seeing him without my glasses brings back a feeling I've had a few times in the past year. The idea that I've made him blush or overwhelmed him – the way girls get sometimes when you give them an unexpected compliment, the way he got when I played with his hair a few minutes ago – makes my chest tighten.

"Anyway," he says. "Eric Draven was played by Brandon Lee, Bruce Lee's son."

"Uh-huh." I feel a little bit of my balance come back so I sit up straight and hold my arms out, twisting my hands as the wind passes over them.

"But he died filming the shoot-out scene. You know, the big one in the warehouse? Something went wrong with the blanks."

"Oh damn," I say, not completely focused on what he's saying, and lost in my own thoughts. "You're so *smart*, dude, it's amazing."

"But…uh, that's why the editing's so weird in…in places. Why it's a little janky."

"I *see*," I say. "I don't think I ever noticed *editing* before. You should go to, like, film school or something."

"I've been thinking about it," he says. "Maybe."

I suddenly can imagine Morgan in New York City or LA, going to some fancy college – writing papers about this sort of thing, lounging with trendy kids on a hill, expounding on film in a way that would go over my head. And maybe fitting in there in a way he never does here. It's almost like I can see it. But then, would that mean he'd leave me behind? Does the University of Tennessee have a film school? Would he even want to go there? Probably not.

With everything being about football this past year, I

105

can barely see further than the next pass I'm going to catch. But say I get into college, and say I go, and say Morgan's not there with me? The thought makes my stomach sink. Worse yet, say I'm trapped in Thebes for ever, and Morgan's the one who leaves…I swallow the bile in my throat and push the thought away.

"I don't know," he says. We sweep through the kudzu-choked roundabout on Lafayette Street. Another long moment passes. I flap my arms slowly. He takes a deep breath.

"So, Jasmine kissed me," he says.

The lights coil and snap into a shape I can't make sense of. What did I decide I shouldn't forget? Something about how Morgan should have been a girl? But he's *not* is the thing, and maybe that thought, that *weird* thought, I realize with a sickening lurch, was just a perverted, roundabout way of wishing I could keep him for ever. If Morgan's a boy, which he *is*, then eventually he'll get a girlfriend and spend more time with her than me. I picture them kissing, their hands under each other's shirts, their thoughts focused on nothing but each other, and my vision swims.

My balance gives out and I start to sway, and suddenly the only thought in my whole skull is this: maybe beer isn't actually great.

I let go of Morgan's chest and go crashing off the bike. Asphalt bites into my arms and I lie on my back, dazed by the spinning street lights, unable to move.

MORGAN

Pedalling suddenly becomes so easy I shoot forward a few yards and slip my foot to the ground, leaving a streak of old sneaker along the asphalt. I'm confused for a second, but then I hear a hard thud and a groan.

I look over my shoulder to see Eric on his back, rolling and holding himself. I drop my bike on the sidewalk and run to him. Stupid. It was *stupid* to tell him about the kiss. It was meaningless anyway. Plus, Jasmine thinks I'm gay now, so it meant less than nothing. But after feeling his face on the back of my neck, and his endless stream of compliments, it was kind of a lot. I felt like a cat who's been petted a little too hard for a little too long, but instead of biting, I dropped a bombshell on my drunk friend. Guilt eats at my insides.

"Hey! Hey." I stumble to a stop next to him and fall to my knees. "Hey. Oh my god, are you okay? Talk to me."

Eric doesn't say anything, just moans and pushes himself to a sitting position. I support his neck and shoulder and look him over, trying to remember what Dad taught me about concussion. I pull Eric's head into my lap, and inspect him. His blond hair drapes across my legs, and his neck is heavy against my thighs. It doesn't look like he's bleeding or anything is broken. I take that as a good sign.

"Are you okay?" I ask again. "Look at me."

Eric grimaces and opens his eyes. Our stares connect, and even though his gaze is marred with pain and alcohol, our eyes meet and something suddenly feels electric between us – adult and quiet – not like our goofy back-and-forth from before. Neither of us can break the stare. It feels like the world slows down and my universe zooms in to this one point. To just stoplights, and the warm asphalt, and us. To me and Eric.

I remember something I haven't thought about in like ten years – we were in preschool and a girl got in trouble for chasing boys and kissing them in the playground. We hadn't even known what kissing was, except a thing that grown-ups did sometimes. Eric and I were little and curious, so the next time I spent the night at his house, when the lights were off and the grown-ups weren't around to get mad at us, I asked Eric if I could kiss him. And we did. And we were five, so it didn't really feel like anything, and we laughed and curled up in bed and went to sleep.

How did I forget that? Now, looking down at him, it seems insane.

My heart won't stop crashing against my ribs. I feel my lips parting, picture my mouth moving the same way Jasmine's did. Was that *tonight*? How was it not a lifetime ago?

I'm just confused. I need to move.

"I…uh…I'm—" Eric starts to say, but the sound of tyres makes him pause.

An SUV rolls up next to us and I look up, tense, as the window rolls down and the Garth Brooks that's blaring on the speakers is turned down.

"Everything okay, young lady?" a man says. I can't make out his face in the dark. I start to say something, but then the fact that he called me a lady hits my sternum and fills me with light and I can't bring myself to let him hear my voice. Luckily Eric sits up straighter and gives the SUV a thumbs-up. I smile and nod in agreement and that seems to satisfy him. The man wishes us a good night and drives off.

"Wow," I say. I start to hook an arm under Eric's to lift him. Whatever that mood was, thank *god* it got interrupted. He places a hand on my shoulder and I keep talking to quiet down my ner ves. "That was weird, right? He thought I was—"

But then Eric's left hand is on the back of my neck and his right is on my hip. There's a breath where our eyes lock and orange light glints in his. I don't really know what's going on, except that I know, kind of distantly, that Eric is looking at me like he wants me, that we aren't five this time, that this electricity in my tailbone, the bottom of my stomach, the back of my neck is how desire is meant to feel. Before I can process it, Eric parts his lips and brings them to mine. I shudder and touch his chest, expecting at first to push away, but then I stop understanding why I would, because his chest is so firm under my fingers and his lips are soft. I fall into him like a drop of wax, and I realize this is how a kiss is supposed to make you feel, and...

But...

An image fills my head. I see myself as I am: a boy with stringy hair and baggy clothes, a boy with peach fuzz on his lip, a boy with more brown hairs sprouting on his chest and stomach every day. My stomach turns and the image shifts and it's just like that video I watched a few months ago, two bulging, veiny men growling as they take each other. Bile rises in my throat and I pull away with a furious wipe of my sleeve across my lips. This feels wrong, even with Eric. *Especially* with Eric. I pull back, my palms firmly on his chest as I push him away. His eyes are wide, and confused, and hurt, and I know in this moment that my face mirrors his – boyish and unsure – wary that everything is about to change.

A few things feel certain: I'm not gay. I'm not straight.

I'm not made to connect to other human beings in that way, and I'm not sure I ever will. I'm just broken.

"What the *hell*, dude?" I say, and the way my voice crackles between deep and normal breaks my heart.

ERIC

"What the *hell*, dude?"

I blink and slowly realize what I've done, the pain and sudden spike of embarrassment pushing me back towards sober. He stands, crinkles his nose, and shoves his hands in his hoodie.

"I…" I rub my temple and slowly rise to my feet. My knees threaten to give out, but I'm too self-conscious to reach out for support. "I'm sorry. I'm drunk, and…and I was confused or something."

"Confused," Morgan says. He strides back to his bike. "Are you gay or what?"

"No," I say. I stumble after him and feel naked down to my nerve endings. "I don't know. I don't know. I like girls, and just…without my glasses you looked…" Even in the dim light I can see his cheeks are crimson when I catch up to him. I think of my brothers and all the homophobic shit that they always say about Morgan. About him being a "sissy" or worse. But here he is and here I am, and maybe it's *me*. I think back to all the times I saw him from the corner of my eye, or without my glasses, or in a moment of vulnerability, and how I felt a snap of desire in my chest, and how hard I've tried *not* to think about it, and…but… it's *only* with Morgan. And Morgan's small, and skinny, and he has long hair. Have I felt this way about Nate? Chud? *Any* of the guys on the football team? I think back, my thoughts unsteady and slurred, and decide that no, I haven't. "I'm not gay."

"Okay…" Morgan says. He picks his bike up and rolls it beside us. He rubs his nose and pulls his hood up even though it's like seventy-five degrees. "Me neither."

"You could tell me, you know," I say. "If you are."

My mind flits back to our kiss for a second. How it felt to have his lips on mine. He leaned in, ever so briefly. It felt like he wanted it as much as I did. He kissed me back. But now I can feel his guard's up – that he's pushing me away. I rub my ribs and flinch at the growing bruise. It hurts where I hit the ground, but the dull pain distracts from the embarrassment, or the tension, or whatever this is.

"I said I'm not," Morgan says. His eyes dart to me and his normally full lips thin into a razor-sharp line. His nostrils flare and he lets out a quick breath, then turns to me. "I know I'm not, like, *normal*. Believe me, I know.

But if I ever figure out the specific way I'm fucked up, I'll tell you."

Maybe I should say it, what I thought when I was behind him on the bike, about how things would be better if he were a girl, about how I can't bear the thought of us falling in love with other people and growing apart. The first revelation seemed so perfect and important, and the second so sobering and desperate, and when I was on the ground, looking up, I knew in a flash that I had to kiss him. It felt like the universe was telling me to.

Night sounds rise up, texturing the space between us with the yearning cries of frogs, crickets and the last of the season's cicadas. I still don't have my glasses. I can still see this blurry, feminine outline of him that just feels right.

I take in a breath, ready to say it again, better and more clearly. Morgan's eyes drift to mine expectantly, but I can't tell him that. I've already acted like enough of an asshole tonight. I can't lose him. What if it's just too weird? What if it's a final straw, and then the last thread joining us together unspools? I let my breath flow out and aim for a casual shrug.

"I don't think you're fucked up," I eventually say instead. I run my hands down my face. I don't want to be drunk any more or ever again. "This is so weird. I'm sorry. I'm never drinking again. Are we…are we still cool?"

Morgan takes another step back and for a minute I

think, that's it. This is how my fourteenth birthday begins and how our friendship ends.

"Neither of us has ever been cool," Morgan says. I look up and his dim smile expands into a grin. "But we're still friends if that's what you mean." The nausea recedes a little, but then he points a finger at me. "*Just* friends. Which means you sleep on the floor tonight."

"And tomorrow we'll pretend it never happened?"

"Right," Morgan says. He turns his face away from the street light and rubs the bridge of his nose with his frayed sleeve. "I'll lock the memory away in a big warehouse with everything else I want to forget. Have my *top men* take care of it."

Half of me is relieved as I hear the words come out of his mouth. But another part, the part that still thinks Thebes is beautiful despite everything, screams that locking away this memory would be like destroying a part of us. But I'm not sure I have a choice.

"Any chance we could watch *Indiana Jones* instead of *The Crow* too?" I ask.

His arm snaps out and pops me in the shoulder. It doesn't hurt, but I make a show of wincing all the same. He winks and sticks his tongue out.

"Don't press your luck, birthday boy."

FIFTEENTH
BIRTHDAY

MORGAN

I wish we had a Sephora here, or even an Ulta. I read online that employees there are usually okay helping people like me. *People like me.* I'm still trying to figure out what that means. But no, apparently neither company saw the profit in setting up a franchise in a town that's been dying since before I was born, so now I'm standing in probably one of the last Kmarts in the country, pretending to be fascinated by cat food while I watch the cosmetics section from the corner of my eye.

I could have gone to Walmart, I guess, but *way* more people I know shop there. Half their employees are either my classmates or they're teachers working nights and weekends – it's the only other place to work around here, unless your family has a farm, or gas stations, or you want to drop out and work at the chicken processing plant. I mean, a lot of kids do it – Oak County's junior and senior classes are way smaller than the freshman and sophomore classes. Around here, graduating from high school is a privilege.

Thankfully, the only person walking the brightly lit aisles of the Kmart is an older woman I don't recognize. But still, I don't want to take any chances. Maybe she goes to the same church as somebody from school. Maybe she's somebody's aunt. It's too risky. I finger the wad of cash and Mom's birthday letter in my hoodie pocket and feel my mouth go dry.

This year, Mom wrote for me to use the money to buy something fun for myself, but the thing is, not much is actually fun any more. It's hard to remember when it started, or maybe it's been building up for a long time and I've tried not to think about it, but over the last year, more and more, everything just feels kind of…grey. Or, maybe not grey. My favourite band is Siouxsie and the Banshees and my favourite movie is *The City of Lost Children*, so grey can be fun.

It's more like everything feels empty, like the world's a video game where you've put in a cheat code only to see that nothing's there – that inside the walls and bodies it's all hollow. The truth is, I spend most of my free time in bed staring at the wall. Even being around Eric is weird.

It was hard to look Eric in the eye for a while after the kiss, no matter how cool I tried to play it. Since then, Eric and a couple of other boys (but mostly Eric) have slipped into my fantasies when I least expect it, which pretty much settles whether I like boys or girls. But I'm not a boy in the fantasies, and when I try to make myself visualize that they fall flat. I know, more than ever, that I'm supposed to be a girl. Or that I'll be happier if I'm a girl. Or that I am a girl. I guess I still don't know the specifics.

Over the summer, when Eric had constant football practice and I was mostly alone, things kept getting worse in my head. I haven't seen him much since school started. And I know that should make me sad, right? But weirdly, I just feel like I'm made of packing peanuts, outside to inside, with a dark little thunderstorm core where my heart should be.

I think I've done a pretty good job hiding all this emptiness from Dad and Eric, but there *was* a pretty huge fight last June, when Dad saw my report card and realized I'd pretty much stopped doing anything but the bare minimum – except in my one elective film and video editing class, which I don't even get graded in.

Faking it around Jasmine's been a little harder, but she does most of the talking when we hang out, so the trick is to nod and ask the right kinds of questions. She's tried asking me about being gay a few more times since the party last year, but every time it comes up I feel emptier than usual and can't stop thinking about her kissing me, and then Eric kissing me, and how sick and weird it all still makes me feel. And I know it's ungrateful to feel like this, but the way she seems *excited* every time she brings it up, like I'm some kind of fun novelty…I don't know. I'm not a project, or at least I'm not *her* project.

But even I know this can't go on for ever, which is why I'm at a stupid freaking Kmart. In the make-up aisle.

My plan is this: get make-up, put it on, look at myself in the mirror, and see how I feel – see if I feel anything at all. Then maybe I'll know how to move forward. Maybe it'll tell me something I need to know.

I can do this, I tell myself, but fear eats at my insides. What if someone sees me? What if this doesn't make me feel better?

Despite what Mom said – that I should use her gift to buy something fun – I know I should spend this money on video editing software, books on directing, acting classes, something like that. And while I want to pursue even more of this movie stuff, I just sort of mindlessly headed this way once the money was in my hand. Partly I told myself it was a test – could I buy something that would make me feel something?

I force myself to focus on the cosmetics in front of me. I don't even bother to look at brand names. Eyeliner, mascara, an eyeshadow palette, and a set of brushes – all of it seems pretty interchangeable, so I just grab at them randomly and throw them into my shopping bag. Blush seems a little harder, because I don't want to look like a clown, but my eyes fall on a peach that looks natural enough. I pick a foundation with a warm base, though who knows if the tone will match. It's not like I can hang out long enough to try them on my wrist like the YouTube tutorials suggested.

As I drop the foundation into my bag, I realize I don't feel bad any more. A little nervous, maybe, but my stomach is calm and I feel warm in my neck and at the base of my spine. Even a little brave. I'm running through my budget while I roll a tube of lip gloss in my palm when a pair of sneakers enters my field of vision and I freeze.

"You're not shoplifting, are you?" a girl says. I squeeze the little plastic cylinder so hard it starts to crack. My mind screams that I should run, but my body stays locked in place. "Store's on its last legs already and I need this job. Steal from Walgreens or something if you're desperate, okay?"

"I'm not—" I say. I want to tell her I'm going to pay for all this, but my voice comes out hoarse and small and I still can't look up. Her feet shift.

"Oh!" she says. "I thought you were a girl."

My shoulders tense and I look up at her. My heart stutters when I realize she goes to my school, that I recognize her from film class. I'm pretty sure her name's Kaleigh. Worse, when my eyes focus and move past her, I realize three of her friends are clustered at the other end of the aisle, watching us with barely contained amusement.

"Morgan?" she says. "From Mr Picket's class, right?"

"Uh," I say. "Yeah."

Her face shifts to an expression somewhere between pity and amusement and she tilts her head.

"So you aren't stealing?" Kaleigh asks innocently.

I shake my head. Her friends audibly snicker and I struggle to keep my expression blank. It's not the worst thing I've experienced this last year by a mile. When Eric isn't eating lunch with me, it's pretty much a constant barrage of french fries, tater tots, harsh whispers of things like "faggot" and "eat shit". I'm lucky if I make it to my lunch table without being tripped, so now I either don't eat or just bring a sandwich in my backpack.

As I stare down four girls from my class in the make-up aisle of a Kmart like a sheriff at high noon, I tell myself I've had it worse. But all the same, I feel my most shameful self laid bare for them to pick at. I hold my shopping bag to my chest and cross my arms over my heart.

"No, I'm not *stealing*," I say to Kaleigh. "I'm. Buying these. For my. For a girl."

"*You've* got a girlfriend?" She flips her hair and looks thoughtful. "Is it that Mexican girl?"

I want to throw my bag at her and yell that Jasmine has a name and she was born in *Georgia* but I can barely move.

"I always kind of figured you and that blond football kid with the glasses were a thing."

I flinch. *That* stings way more than I want it to. It brings up the idea that our kiss last year might have

124

unlocked something more in me. In some of my fantasies, we're grown up and we have a home together. Maybe he's a famous musician and I'm on the road with him. I know it's so stupid, and I always feel dirty after, but I also suddenly hate Kaleigh for tapping into something I was so sure people couldn't see. Eric is untouchable. And me – I'm nobody.

"We *aren't*," I say. My mouth feels so dry. "And the make-up isn't. It's not for me."

"Okay, whatever," Kaleigh says with a shrug. I back away until I'm out of the aisle then practically run to the self-checkout. I feed bills into the checkout machine with trembling hands, praying that they'll all be accepted and I won't have to ask the attendant for help. My prayers are answered, just this once, and I walk out of the store as fast as I can without actually running, the make-up clinking in my backpack like so many priceless jewels.

The sun breaks through a slate-grey cloud canopy as I mount my bike, and once my blood is up from pedalling and I'm on the road, the girls' laughter feels distant, just another hurt among a hundred that've already scabbed over. It doesn't matter. I'll barely remember them tomorrow.

I adjust the shoulder straps of my backpack to make sure the make-up is secure, then zip onto a side street, not exactly happy, but vibrating with the knowledge that at least I'm finally doing *something*.

ERIC

Sweat courses down my back and chest as I make my way to the locker room after football practice. The showers are blessedly empty when I trudge in, panting and weak-legged, though the air is still thick with humid, sweaty stickiness.

I check my phone and don't find any messages from Morgan, which is weird, since we're supposed to have birthday plans tonight.

I turn the shower tap to full cold and rush in. After the initial shock, the chill seeps into my muscles and loosens up all the knots and kinks.

I like to sing when I shower; the acoustics on tile are good, and since I've basically stopped playing guitar, it's the only time I really do it. I sing "Sing Me Spanish Techno" by The New Pornographers, off their album *Twin Cinema* – the last CD I bought before sort of losing interest in music. I'm on the line about listening too long to one song when I reach up to shampoo my hair and, not for the first time, consider trimming at least a little bit off. It's getting long enough that my helmet fits weird, but it's one of my last little acts of rebellion against Dad, now that I'm his perfect football prodigy at just fifteen.

Maybe things would be better if Peyton hadn't left so suddenly. He fell in love with a train kid who'd floated through town on her way to Bonnaroo, and he ditched the end of his senior year to run away with her. Peyton hasn't contacted us since, not even Isaac, and Dad's made it clear that my brother won't be welcome home under any circumstances.

Now Dad's gaze is on me 24/7, as if he's watching for whatever went wrong with Peyton to sour in me too. I didn't even have Isaac to lean on over the summer. Apparently, he wanted to stretch his wings before his last year of college, so he got an apartment in Knoxville. I asked if I could see it back in June, just to escape Dad's eagle eyes for a weekend, but Isaac hemmed and hawed about the gas cost to drive out and pick me up. I know enough to know when I'm not wanted.

Usually I'd have spent the summer glued at the hip with Morgan, but…well, it hasn't been great between us, so it's not a total surprise that I haven't heard from him yet today. When we hang out, he spends more and more time staring off into space with his knees pulled to his chest.

I feel like I should press him about what's wrong, but when has that ever worked before with him? At this point, he'll tell me when he feels like telling me, right?

The shower's water pressure dies. With a heavy sigh, I cut the song short, finish washing quickly, and get dressed.

Nate and Chud come charging towards me from the parking lot when I step outside the gym. Chud's grown into his mass in the last year, leaving him a wall of meat with no rounded edges – the perfect linebacker.

"Happy fuckin' birthday, faggot!" Chud says, pulling me into a headlock and tousling my hair. The word hits me like a bat to the head. Every time they yell that something's gay or I'm a fag I get a little jolt of panic. I flash back to a year ago, to that kiss in the street, and then I squeeze my eyes shut, fill my thoughts with static, and chase those feelings away. The *only* people I've ever been attracted to besides Morgan are girls. I was drunk. I'm not gay.

"Fuck off," I say to Chud, but I'm laughing as I twist my way out of his grip and slap the back of his head.

"You didn't think we'd forget, did you?" Nate says, flipping his car keys with one hand while his other holds his duffel bag over his shoulder. "Those legs took us to state. Like hell we'd forget."

"Shucks," I say. I pop my back and grin. "I didn't know y'all's feelings ran so deep."

"Don't make it weird," Chud says, but Nate just flashes that winning smile and shakes his head as he drops his duffel, opens it, and pulls out a six-pack of Budweiser and a rolled-up magazine.

"Here!" Nate says, tossing me the magazine. It's held by a rubber band so it doesn't flutter open, but when I catch it and examine it I can just make out the word "Penthouse" on the cover. A longer glance reveals it's faded and curling at the corners, and the woman on the front has big, eighties hair and airbrushed make-up that makes me think, of all things, of my grandparents' old photo albums from before I was born. I feel a blush forming, but then I cough it away.

Nate claps my shoulders and solemnly says, "Just don't think about us while you yank your pud, okay?" then pulls me into a one-armed hug. "There's another six-pack with your name on it at Connor's tonight, by the way, so save this one for later."

"I'll come if I can," I say, hoping I don't sound ungrateful. Morgan should take priority on our birthday, but Morgan also should have gotten back to me.

"You'll have to break yourself away from your pet queer, of course," Nate says. My fingers tighten around the magazine. Everything in my body screams for me to say, *Don't call him that*, but I can't do it – unless I want to be his bodyguard full-time, standing up for him will probably just get him hassled more, and too much of my home life is riding on me remaining the golden boy to risk it. "You guys don't have a date planned, right?"

"Jealous?" I say, though I realize I still haven't heard back from Morgan.

"You wish," Nate says. "Speaking of, I think Susan's looking for you, says she has a present with your name on it. Work your game right and maybe you'll lose the V card."

"Gross," I say, not realizing until after I say it that he'll think I'm calling sex with a girl gross.

"Knew you were gay," Chud says.

"Fuck off," I say.

"Girls, girls," Nate says, holding his hands up as if to keep us apart. "Let's not squabble, yeah? Save that energy for Connor's. Anyway, Eric, we gotta go. Places to be and people to do, you know how it goes."

"Yeah. Thanks for this," I say. Chud makes a jerking-off motion, I guess referencing the magazine I'm now stuck holding on school grounds, and I briefly wonder which charm school he attended before waving goodbye.

I stow the magazine in my bag and make my way to where my bike is chained up. I sing under my breath as I walk, hoping nobody hears me. I'm so tired from practice that I nearly bump into Susan when I round the corner to the bike rack.

"Boo!" she says. She bounces forwards and I stumble back a few steps. Susan is tall and lean – now the tallest girl on the cheer squad – with a face made of long, curving lines and a mouth that always seems a little puckered up, like she's thinking of something she's not sure she should say. Her long, black ponytail trails behind her like a ribbon as she sways back and forth, grinning, her hands hidden behind her.

"Susan!" I say. I drop my bag and nudge it behind me as if she might somehow sense what's inside it.

"Me!" Susan says. She leans against the wall and looks coy. It's always good news when a girl looks coy, at least I imagine it is, and coy looks especially good on Susan. I've suspected we've been flirting for most of the past year, but girls remain a mystery to me, and I haven't figured out how to follow through on it. "How was practice?" she asks.

"Uh," I say. So charming. "Good? It was good. Coach Tyler says I might make varsity next—"

"When were you gonna tell me today's your birthday?" she says, leaning in, upgrading her expression from coy to mischievous.

"Never?" I say with a shrug. "I don't really like birthday stuff." Unless it's with Morgan, but every time I admit that to someone, it feels a little like social suicide.

"Well, *too bad*!" she says, whipping her hand around and brandishing a cupcake covered in purple-and-red frosting with a totally cute-hokey "15" candle stuck on top.

"Whoa!" I say. I back up a step and laugh. The candle's actually lit. "How did you not burn yourself?"

"A girl has to have her secrets," she says. "Blow it out!" I do as I'm told while she sings, "Happy birthday to you," and it's so cute, and I'm blushing so hard that I'm really glad the guys aren't here and school is mostly deserted.

"Susan," I say. "Thanks. Thank you so much. Should I eat it now?"

"You're not gonna carry it all the way home on your bike."

"True," I say. She laughs. I smile. I unwrap the cupcake, toss the wrapper into the nearest garbage can, and take a bite. "Did you make this yourself?" I try to say, but my mouth is full so it's mostly mumbles and a spray of crumbs.

"Yup!" she says, somehow interpreting me. "And I've got another present when you're done."

"Susan," I say as I remove the candle, lick it clean, and shove it in my pocket; I'm not going to just *throw it away* in front of her. "This is crazy." We have geometry, chemistry, and English together, and we sit by each other in all of them. She helps me with science and maths, and I help her with English. Susan makes me laugh all the time, and football and cheerleading are kind of adjacent, so maybe I shouldn't be so surprised that we've gotten this close, but I am.

"Ready for your next present?"

"Sure," I say. I lean with one hand on the wall in a way

I hope looks cool. Then she takes a step forward, leans in, and kisses me on the cheek.

Susan's blushing crimson as she steps back, but her voice is bold as she says, "Maybe I'll see you at Connor's?"

I watch, feeling distant, as she brushes a strand of hair out of her face and chews her lip. Tonight's nebulous plans with Morgan evaporate in an instant.

"Definitely," I reply. "See you there."

MORGAN

I pat my face dry like the girl in the YouTube video told me to and stand before the bathroom mirror with my eyes closed.

I admit to myself that my plan terrifies me. What if I see myself and I like it? What if it makes me happy? But… what if I put on the make-up and everything stays the same and I keep wanting to disappear? What if there's no way out of this and there never will be? What happens if when I die they bury me in a suit and tie?

In order to do this properly, I'm going to have to look at myself, but my hair's up in a ponytail and that means I have to see my face without anything to hide its shape. I take one breath, then another, and open my eyes.

A sad-looking boy stares back at me. I try to be objective about his appearance, because I want this whole exercise to be as scientific as possible. He has good cheekbones, full lips, big eyes, and nice olive skin without too many blemishes, but his nose is too big and round at the tip, there's a faint shadow of hair growing on his upper lip and along the edges of his jaw. Dark circles have formed under his eyes from never sleeping, and his forehead is too high, the brown hair already receding the littlest bit – or is that just in my head? His eyebrows are way too thick. It could be worse. The boy staring back at me only barely qualifies as a boy. He's pretty androgynous. Scarily thin, if his grandma is to be believed, and his collarbones *do* poke out pretty far. Who knows how long before puberty ruins everything, though? The thought makes my stomach lurch again.

Okay, step one of the experiment – the inspection – is done. I breathe. My shoulders rise and fall. I've got time to do this without freaking out. Dad should be at practice for another hour, and then he'll probably hang out for a while afterwards with the assistant coach.

My phone buzzes and I see a new text from Eric – a sort of wishy-washy abandonment of our plans, but it's fine because I was going to cancel anyway. I need to do this.

I read back over my handwritten notes that I took down as I secretly watched a few YouTube make-up videos at school. Step 1: Wash your face and pat dry. Check. Step 2: Apply primer. I rummage in the Kmart bag and groan when I realize I forgot to get primer. It'll probably be okay though, right? Step 3: Apply foundation. It takes a minute to get the plastic off, and then I accidentally squirt foundation on my shirt, but after a minute or two I've got a nice little glob on the back of my left hand and I'm ready to go. I follow the movements of the girl from the YouTube video as best as I remember, dabbing foundation on first and then blending out from the centre of my face in big, round motions. I look silly at first and there's a moment I wonder if I'm doing it wrong, but then it all smoothes out and my breath catches.

I look like a girl. Or, I mean, I'm *starting* to. Mostly right now I look like a girl ghost, but even that's enough to make my neck tingle and my muscles relax in a way that's mostly foreign. I take a step back and look at myself. The faint shadow of facial hair is gone. The harsh angles around my nose are softened. The dark circles around my eyes are still there but a little brighter. I smile and realize that I haven't done so in probably months and that my smile is pretty in a timid, nervous way. Next comes eyeshadow, which I copy from the pattern on the back of the little plastic case. Nothing fancy, just tan and brown and an understated gold shimmer – I want to look like a girl my age, not a prostitute or a drag queen. Not that there's anything wrong with being those things, I guess, just…that doesn't feel like me.

Part of me starts planning for my next trip to the store, for buying black lipstick and grey eyeshadow and pulling off a *real* goth look, and I get so excited I don't even really notice how uncomfortable it feels jamming these brushes all over my eyelids. Eyeliner is even less comfortable. My lines are messy and there's no way I can pull off wings yet, but it makes my eyes look bigger all the same and that's nice.

The YouTube girl said to use an eyelash curler, which I chose not to get because they looked like medieval torture devices. I've got thick eyelashes anyway. I try to stop myself from blinking as I brush mascara on. Next is blush, which is a little tricky because *this* girl said to smile and trace a "U" under the apple of my cheek, but other things I've watched have said to stick to the top of my cheekbone. I just sort of rub it on and hope for the best – it's subtle enough that the end result looks okay.

I'm a little dazed as I try to concentrate on my transformed face. I want to get an idea of what I look like, a real *objective* idea, like when I looked myself over before, but my eyes won't focus. My fingers feel numb and they're shaking. I have to brace my elbow to put on lip gloss. And then I rub the excess off on the back of my hand, smack my lips, step back, and let my eyes take in my whole reflection.

And there she is.

I touch my jaw and she touches hers. I watch her lips part in awe and, for the first time in a long time, it's not in a tight frown. She blinks slowly. I blink slowly. Because this is me.

All I can do is stare. At some point the stretched-out neckline of my ratty thrift store shirt slipped off my shoulder. A strand of hair falls across my face. A girl who could be my sister stares back at me – it's not even that I did a good job with the make-up, because I didn't, but she's *there*.

There's a surge of vertigo as I realize *this* is what it's like to bridge the gap between me-the-body and me-the-self. Or the start of it. It feels like waves are crashing in my ears, warm foam rising up to envelop me. I wrap my arms around my stomach and take a long, clean breath. And that's really it – I feel *clean* for the first time in years. I feel—

Whatever epiphany I was closing in on shatters when I hear the front door open and Dad's heavy footfalls down the hall. Of all the days for him to come home early, of course it's today. I scramble, trying to shove all the make-up out of sight, but mostly dropping it on the floor. I kick what's visible behind the toilet. I'm hyperventilating and it's hard to think. I have to wash my face. *I have to wash my face.*

Shit. Shit. Shit.

"Hey, bud?" Dad calls. I hear him puttering somewhere between the main area and the kitchen. "You home? I cut practice short so I could get us a birthday dinner. You still like Chinese, right?"

"Yeah!" I say. My voice cracks, displaying how it's deepened – yet another act of betrayal. "Yeah. Yeah. Cool.

Bathroom. Uh." I run the tap hot and grab a washrag. "Minute. Be out in a minute."

"Take your time. Got a surprise when you get out!"

I make do with the hand soap, but even when I scrub so hard my skin hurts all it does is smudge everything. I blink the water out of my eyes and look up to find a panic-stricken raccoon staring back at me in the mirror. Make-up wipes. I was supposed to buy fucking make-up wipes. And of course he came home early. It's my birthday. How could I be so stupid? Except I guess I'm a broken, stupid person, so maybe it's not surprising at all. Everything's going to be ruined. And all for what, for this mental illness? This fetish? This…this *whatever* this is?

I slam the heel of my hand into the sink, and a bolt of pain shoots up to my elbow. I yell in frustration, and that's all it takes to break me. The roiling thunderstorm in my chest crackles forth, the one always rumbling *just* under the layer of numbness. I hold onto the sides of the sink and feel my breathing go ragged and hot.

My mouth peels apart and a guttural scream comes out. I open my eyes, only to see my reflection glaring back at me, this *disgusting* body again, always, and for ever. Before I know what I'm doing, I cock my arm and punch, then again, then a third time, crunching glass drowning out my voice.

It wouldn't be so bad if I could just stop thinking about it. About what a freak I am.

Freak.

I hear footsteps in the hallway. Through my blurred vision I notice blood dripping from my knuckles. I smear it on my pants and hiss fire through clenched teeth. Dad pounds at the door. Why can't I just be *normal*? I think back to the drawings from last year, to all the futures Mom imagined for me, and I can feel them sloughing off with every second I keep wallowing in this. Dad *keeps* pounding and I feel the vibration inside my skull. He's going to break the door.

"*What?*" I scream.

"Morgan!" Dad says. "What the hell's goin' on in there?"

"Nothing!"

"Don't lie to me," Dad says. "Open the door."

"No," I shout. "Go away."

"Morgan, hey," Dad says, his voice taking on a softer tone. "Whatever it is, we can...we can talk about it. I know you've been stressed, and I've tried to give you space, but you're still my son."

God.

"*Go away.*"

"Morgan, please," Dad says. I want him to yell. Part of me, a deep, animal part, wants him to kick the door down, notice the make-up under the sink, put two and two together, and force me to confess. The rest of me notices the quiver in his voice and it tells me, not for the first time,

140

that I'm the worst thing that's ever happened to everyone I love.

"GO AWAY!"

"You're all I've got left," he finally says, his voice catching.

All I've got left.

All I've got left.

I don't say anything, just press my back to the wall and slide down until I'm sitting with my face buried in my knees.

"I…listen, I know I haven't been the best dad since… since everything. I know you've needed me, and I haven't…I mean. I'm here. Now. If you wanna talk."

My lips part a fraction of an inch, but then, as my thoughts stumble through the wreckage of this breakdown, a memory I haven't thought of in years catches my attention. I was nine, maybe ten, and it was past my bedtime but I couldn't sleep. I wanted a glass of milk and an Oreo, so I snuck through the living room, behind the couch where Mom and Dad sat, her watching a late-night talk show while he scribbled plays in his big red binder. And as I was coming back from the kitchen, unnoticed as usual, something on the show caught my eye.

I peeked around the couch, cookie hanging from my teeth, and saw one of the men running for *something* – president, maybe – say that of *course* he would consider nominating a gay person to the Supreme Court, not only that, but a lesbian, a bisexual, or even a transgender person. I didn't know what transgender meant, but I *felt* what it meant, and I knew part of me felt good to hear a man that important say something like that. But then the host grinned and said, "All rise for the Honourable Justice Chick with Dick!" and the live audience laughed, and my little stomach twisted into knots, and then Mom snickered, and a snort of amusement escaped from Dad.

Even if I tell him, even if he pretends to be okay with my secret, I think I've always known I can never, ever forget that deep down, under any smiles and encouragement, he'll think I'm a joke. A frivolous, useless, hilarious person who could never be something like a judge or a director or…or anything, I guess, but a "chick with a dick", which I found out much later is a porn term on top of being a punchline. But the other part of me is so tired of feeling this way. Of being alone.

I decide to test him, to give him *one* chance to push through the cobwebs, to show me he knows me even a little.

"I've just been really lonely," I say through the door.

"I get that," Dad says.

I rub my temple and sniff. "Maybe…maybe I should get back into sports."

This is *not* me. But this is the me he wants. I know it is.

"Really?" Dad says. There's a note of joy in his voice, like a kid on Christmas morning.

"Mm. Get some exercise. Spend more time with you and Eric."

Tell me no, I want to scream at him. Tell me you don't think I can handle that kind of commitment and I need therapy. Sit me down and make me tell you what's wrong, because no way are you stupid enough to believe *this* is the solution.

"Well!" Dad says. My shoulders sag and as the last bits of rage ebb away I feel the old pressure behind my eyes. The numbness returns. "Well, I think that's a *great* idea. Fantastic! If we start workin' you hard you might even be ready for varsity next season."

I sniffle, throw the make-up back in the Kmart bag, and stand on wobbly legs. The make-up is gone, but I still feel its mark upon my face. Dad smiles when I open the bathroom door, but then I walk past him, eyes dead, and stride down the hall towards the door.

"Hey," he says. "Good. Now let's eat, okay?"

"I'm not hungry," I say as I wrench the front door open.

"Where are you going?"

"Out," I say. He starts to argue, but I slam the door, unchain my bike, and ride off into the twilight.

ERIC

"You're here!" Susan says, beaming and hopping up and down as I walk my bike into Connor's yard and prop it next to his garage. She runs to me, and when she hugs me she smells like a fancy candle store and, I mean…it's a lot. I hug her back and cover my pounding heart with a laugh.

"Of course," I say. "Why wouldn't I be?"

Twelve of my teammates are here, with ten cheerleaders interspersed. Connor lives on my side of town, and you can tell. Everyone sits on fancy patio furniture around an expensive-looking firepit, while Lil Wayne blasts from the sound system. Nate already has a girl in his lap and another next to him, both stuck on his every word. Chud has a ring of empties around his chair. They both look up and cheer as Susan and I approach.

Connor jogs over and pulls me into a back-slapping hug. He's taller than me, almost taller than Chud, but lean and with a stubbled face that's mature enough for a college freshman, rather than a high school senior. He's taken me under his wing and sometimes feels more like a big brother to me than Isaac or Peyton.

"Dude!" Connor says, pushing me out to arm's length and looking me up and down. I adjust my glasses and give him a confused look and he laughs. "Why'd I have to find out it's your birthday from *those* jackasses?" He jerks his thumb towards Nate and Chud, who cup their hands around their mouths and howl. Susan snorts and Connor just shakes his head.

"I don't know," I say with a shrug. "Aren't birthdays for little kids?" He wraps an arm around my shoulder and tousles my hair as the three of us walk towards the firepit.

"Just enjoy it while you can," he says. "Now hold tight, I've got something for you." He runs inside and I take the empty chair next to Chud. Suddenly, to my surprise, Susan's bare thighs are on my leg and her arm is around my shoulder. I look up, hoping I'm not blushing too hard, only to find her cheeks turning pink and her eyes dancing nervously.

"Is this okay?" she asks.

"Yeah," I say. I wrap an arm around her waist, pull her close. "Yeah, this is great."

"Your attention please!" Connor says. The music cuts off and everyone looks up to find him crossing the yard with a twelve-pack of hard lemonade tucked under each arm. "Let me first say happy birthday to Oak County High's finest wide receiver in years, Eric McKinley." Cheers rise from all around the fire and I'm torn between the desire to disappear into myself and the urge to bask in the attention.

Connor drops the drinks next to the almost-empty cooler and places his iPod Nano into a dock by the speakers. "And, second, in honour of our youth, I dedicate tonight to immaturity and guilty pleasures. Bitch beers for everyone, and the playlist is open to anyone who isn't afraid to let us know what they sing in the shower."

The guys all groan, but before he can even finish most of the girls have huddled around the iPod, and within moments the backyard is awash in Lady Gaga and Taylor Swift, music I sort of love, but would never be caught dead listening to in public. When the sun sets we're all sore from laughing at the music and have a comfortable buzz from the drinks.

"Truth or dare!" someone yells, and before I can figure out who it was, everyone is chanting "yes". Connor stands and holds his arms out.

"All right, losers," he says. "I'll start." His pointer finger drifts in an arc around the fire, before finally settling on Nate, who needs to be elbowed to pull his attention away from the girl he's making out with. I'm pretty sure her name is Adria. Nate blinks blearily and then grins when he realizes what's happening.

146

"Dare," he says.

"Of course." Connor scratches his chin. "Make out with Chud for a solid minute, with tongue."

And there's the kiss again, always lurking at the back of my mind: Morgan above me, long hair framing his face, lips parted and eyes wide, outlined in white and gold as the moon and street light intermingled. Just like always, a little kernel of desire slips free, knocks around places I don't want.

What am I? What *am* I?

I humour the idea of kissing Chud, even as a joke, and feel uncomplicated revulsion. It was a mistake. Morgan looked like a girl. I was drunk. And everyone is giggling, so clearly amused by the idea of a boy kissing another boy. My mouth feels dry.

"Sure," Nate says. The girl hops out of his lap and Nate stands and stretches. I'm genuinely shocked. Nate must notice my expression. He clicks his tongue and runs his hands down his hips. "I'm a modern man, I'm secure in my sexuality, and I never back down from a challenge." He winks at Chud, whose face pales. "Now c'mere, stud." A deafening peal of laughter rises around the fire as Chud stands fast enough to flip his chair and hops away from Nate's approach. "Come on, dude, I'm not used to getting turned down!" Nate teases.

"This is fucked up," Chud says. "How come I have to do some gay shit if it's his turn?" Nate jumps onto Chud's back, licks his cheek, and purrs, "It's only gay if you pop a boner, dude. You scared you'll like it?"

"Fine," Connor says. "Chud has a point. I've got another idea: give Adria a lap dance. You down, Adria?"

Adria rolls her eyes, smiles, and takes Nate's vacant seat, draping an arm over the back of the chair, slouching, and spreading her legs like the sleaziest country boy imaginable.

"I need some music," Nate says. He hops off Chud's back and jogs to the iPod. A few seconds later, Usher blasts out of the sound system and Nate makes his way towards Adria, bouncing and shaking his hands like he does before every game.

Part of me thinks he's going to play it off as a joke, or just spend the whole song making out with her or grinding on her lap, but then his hips start moving and the laughter around the fire goes quiet as we all remember how competitive Nate can get. The intensity of the moment shifts my attention from Morgan, and then Susan shifts her weight in my lap and something *else* is on my mind, images of *her* moving like that for me, thoughts of what she might look like without clothes by lamplight, by starlight, by firelight. *This* is good, and even better – it's uncomplicated. I wrap an arm around her waist and she leans against my shoulder. Her body pressing into mine is an easy bliss.

Four minutes later, Adria has practically melted into

her chair and the spell breaks as a raucous chorus of cheers and laughter rise up. Nate takes a bow, grabs his drink off the ground, and sits in her lap without even bothering to find his shirt.

"Maybe a real challenge next time, yeah?" he says and then points to me.

"All right, *birthday boy*, truth or dare?"

"Dare," I say, because I'm certain if I pick truth he'll just ask something mean about Morgan.

"Shave your head," Nate says, and I feel as if he's dropped a bucket of ice water on my head.

"Wait," I say. "Wait, no, is it too late to pick truth?"

"Boo!" Nate says. He throws an empty and it arcs super wide. "Coward! All my friends are cowards!"

"Rules are rules," Connor says. "But before we do the deed, how about you actually let it down for once?" Susan hops off my lap and I stand, take a deep breath, and let my hair out of its bun. A bunch of the girls gasp and I'm quickly surrounded by cheerleaders running their fingers through my mane – except, I notice, for Susan, who stands off to the side and watches with an amused look.

"It's not greasy at all," Adria says. "I thought guy hair was always greasy."

I shrug, not sure what to say.

"Gay," Chud says. "You look like a girl."

"He *looks* like a guy with a girlfriend." Adria sneers at him. I exchange a look with Susan, who seems pleased

149

with that description. Adria turns back to me. "This has to be like twelve inches. I bet you could donate it to that charity that makes wigs for sick kids."

"That's a thing?" I say.

"They gave my cousin a wig when she went through chemo," she says. The little reminder of Donna still stings, even after all these years. How much worse must it be for Morgan? "Just cut it off in a ponytail and I'll donate it for you."

"Okay," I say, then Susan and Connor lead me into the house.

Everything happens in a daze. Suddenly I'm on a chair in Connor's bathroom, my shirt off, a towel around my neck. Susan rubs my shoulders and whispers encouragement. I squeeze my eyes shut, too afraid to see my reflection, and then, with a metallic snip, my head feels at least a pound lighter. Susan places something soft and silky in my hands. I look down to see *my* hair shining under the bathroom light. I swallow, take a deep breath, and realize I feel pretty okay with it. At least it'll help some kid.

"Wanna see how it looks before we shave the rest?" Connor says. I squeeze my eyes shut again and shake my head, my cheeks burning.

"You're being really brave," Susan says. She slips her hand into mine and kisses my cheek. "I would be *sobbing* right now."

150

"Thanks," I say. We both flinch and then laugh as Connor produces a huge electric trimmer and turns it on, its industrial buzz rattling the small space. A few terrible minutes later he turns it off again, whips the towel off my shoulders, and hands me a mirror. I take a deep breath and hold it up, and I'm glad I'm sitting down because a feeling of light-headedness hits me when I realize I don't recognize the person looking back at me. I run my fingers over my pale scalp, taking in the odd bumps and lumps I never noticed before, and to my horror I realize I'm about to cry, but then Susan takes my face in her hands and kisses me – my first real, true kiss since Morgan – and I forget everything else.

"You look so much better," she says.

MORGAN

I let my bike fall to the ground when I reach the dumpster. The Kmart bag strikes asphalt and bursts, spilling make-up across the dark pavement. Swearing under my breath, I turn on my phone flashlight and slowly pick up the pieces, one by one, until both my hands are full. I stand there for a moment, in the reeking lot behind the Shell station near our trailer, staring into the dumpster's black maw and listening to night frogs, and I consider not doing this.

It felt good to see that face in the mirror, covered in make-up, if just for a moment, if only the one time. *Amazing*, actually. I recognized her and she felt like me. She *was* me.

But how good would it feel if I put on make-up like that every day? And how bad would it feel if Dad couldn't look at me any more?

Like an idiot, I had allowed myself to fantasize about living in a place like New York or Atlanta or Los Angeles, where both my parents were still alive and so sensitive that I didn't even need to *tell* them. I let myself imagine alternative presents and impossible futures where I could be with someone like Eric as more than a friend. I let myself pretend I lived in a universe where my body was completely different from the one I currently exist in.

But, no.

"Wanting" to be a girl? It's stupid. It's stupid and *insane*.

I live in Thebes, Tennessee. And no one here is down with that "queer shit". I'm trapped in the life I have, and I need to shut down any other fantasy before it hurts me even more. I *want* to make movies. I *want* a new bike. I *want* to not be sick in the head.

I whip the make-up over the dumpster and into the darkness. My throat starts to close. I hear something shatter and I close my eyes.

This way that I feel, this…obsession, it's not a thing that I want and it's not a thing that I am, it's something I *have*. Like a disease. Mom had cancer. I have *autogynephilia* – I saw that word online. Lots of people hate that idea and say it's transphobic, that it makes it a disease, but this *feels* like a disease.

I remember the exact moment I realized Mom was sick, the moment I could hear her crying even out in the waiting room. I was young, but you never forget a moment like that, even if you don't know exactly what's happening. I learned a new word. "Cancer."

And now I have word for myself. Autogynephile. It's like I have a genetic disease I was born with, like how mom's cells were programmed to kill her. Conversion therapy doesn't work. I read that. There's no way to feel better, except living your life like a woman, which is the one thing I can't bear to do. Maybe I can't stand the possibility of losing Dad's or Eric's respect. Maybe I don't want to be reduced to a sex object and it kind of seems, from the outside, like that's all the world would let me be. I feel, with total clarity, that this is going to kill me.

I scream at the top of my lungs, feeling lost and like I don't know where to turn. Where do I go from here? I bend at the waist and buckle my knees. If this were an anime or an action movie, my rage would whip around me like wind, and mournful music would rise up. But my life is neither of those things. This is just a night in the life of a small, lonely, sick kid who wants, more than anything else, to go to sleep and not wake up again.

I hurl the last of the make-up into the dumpster with a crash.

"Kid!"

I'm crouching now, punching the asphalt. My scream has petered out into a rasping croak. A wad of trash hits my side, forcing me to look up, my eyesight blurry.

"Hey, kid! What the hell?"

I see the gas station attendant standing at the outermost edge of the awning lights, looking at me like I'm a crazy person, which I guess I am. I sniffle and run my forearm across my nose.

"You okay? What happened?"

"Nothing," I say. It sounds like I'm getting over a cold.

"You sure? I feel like I should call somebody. Why don't you come inside?"

"Fuck off," I say. I don't need his help.

The gas station attendant flips me the bird and yells for me to be gone in five minutes or he'll call the cops. I pour myself onto my bike and stare into space for a moment, trying to figure out how to get to Eric's house from here, then it hits me he might not even be home. It's his birthday too. What if he's still out celebrating without me? With his new friends? I push the thought away before it can make me feel ill. I don't care. I need to see him.

I pull out my phone to call him and groan when I realize it's dead. Whatever. I'll bike there and figure things out as I go. If I stay alone with my thoughts one second longer I'm afraid something terrible will happen.

The ride itself is mostly a blur. There's a buzzing sound in my head and my muscles refuse to relax. When I finally arrive at his house I don't even feel tired – but something deep inside feels like it's been strained to its breaking point.

All the windows are dark, but who cares? I don't think

I care about anything right now. It must be after his curfew though, so he *should* be home.

"Dude," I hiss. I throw a piece of gravel at Eric's second-floor window. "Dude, come on, I need you."

I keep this up for I don't know how long, maybe an hour, maybe ten minutes, when finally I hear Eric's voice. But it's coming from behind me, on the road.

"Morgan?" he says.

I turn around and there, where before there was only empty road, is Eric. He's frozen, mid-dismount, in a flickering puddle of orange light. Moths flutter above him like a grey halo and somewhere, distant, a night bird lets loose a single lonely note.

But then I squint and lean forwards because something's wrong – he has Eric's bike, and he sounds like Eric, but his head is completely shaved, except for a thin layer of blond fuzz. It can't be him, because Eric loves his hair too much to cut it off. It's the last rock and roll holdout his dad allows him. But then he rolls his bike into the driveway, and I see it really is him.

"Holy shit," he says. "Morgan. Are you okay?"

"Where's your hair?" I say in return, my voice hoarse. But looking at him settles the rough wheezing in my chest. Just the sight of his face makes me immediately feel calmer. And not that I would tell *him*, but the shaved look is kind of nice. It makes me realize how handsome he's becoming every day. God, I'm gross.

Eric grimaces at my comment, running a hand over his head as he walks his bike into the garage. "You didn't become a skinhead and not tell me, right?" I put my hands on my hips, feeling myself come back into my body. "And if you *are* a skin please tell me you're the hardcore kind and not the Nazi kind."

"Black Flag is borderline unlistenable," he says, joining me in the driveway, "and my girlfriend is Jewish. So, no to both."

"Girlfriend?" I say. "Since when do you have a girlfriend?" He arches an eyebrow and I realize that was probably not the best way to ask that question.

"Since tonight, I guess," he says with a shrug, and I feel a flash of jealousy for Susan before I push it away. It's all so easy for him: just like that he suddenly has a girlfriend, and I'm over here like a walking disaster with stupid waterproof mascara stained under my eyes.

"Right, okay, girlfriend. Cool. And what about the hair?" I ask.

"I got dared to shave my head. Does it look stupid?"

"What?" I say. "No. You look…" I shrug. "You look good."

He smiles ruefully. "You *just* asked if I was a Nazi," he says.

"I mean, I wasn't expecting it." I sniffle and rub at my nose with my sleeve. He looks so different – more grown up, manly, yet still Eric. I picture myself with hair that

short. He's growing up into a man, and I'm turning into…
what?

The more I look at Eric the more I wonder why I can't
be normal like him. And then a little voice echoes out of
the dark recesses of my brain, hissing, *Have you ever* really
*tried it? Even when you were little, you never fully committed,
sneaking home to watch movies about princesses and listening
to Mom's dance music. You liked the make-up, but have you
ever* really *tried to be normal…?*

If I can't be a girl, then maybe I should really try being
a boy – to lean in to what I said to Dad. The football
player, the perfect son. Maybe if I pretend, it'll come true.
Maybe I could be someone people won't look away from
or laugh at in the make-up aisle of a Kmart. Someone like
Eric. The football player with a girlfriend, though it's hard
to imagine wanting that last part very much.

Could I do it? If I can't be *with* Eric, then maybe I can
be him? It sounds crazy, I know it does, but maybe…

"Well," Eric says, taking in my silence. "Let's go inside
and you can tell me why you've been crying."

With a nod, I rub my nose and follow him inside,
feeling like an unwashed peasant as I step into his family's
polished, glimmering house. I know abstractly that this
place used to feel like a second home to me, but with Eric's
busy schedule and Carson's constant, simmering
insinuation that he doesn't want me around, that memory
is distant. Only Jenny still seems to like me, checking in

158

occasionally on how Dad and I are faring and making spaghetti whenever I come over, but lately I never know if she's even going to be home, not that I can blame her. "I thought your parents had a rule about having friends over when they're not home. I didn't see their cars…"

"You know you're family," he says as we make our way to the kitchen, then he smiles. It's hard not to be warmed by the lie. "And that rule only applies to girls anyway."

That hits me in the chest like a kick from an angry horse. I keep my face from moving, but my throat closes and tears start bubbling up again. Luckily his back is turned to me as he rummages in the kitchen.

"Sorry for bailing earlier," he says. "But I was actually coming to find you, if you can believe it." I don't say anything, but focus instead on willing this feeling away. He keeps talking without looking up. "It's weird, I know, but I get this, like, pressure at the base of my neck sometimes. Who knows? Maybe it's brain damage. But I always take it as a sign to—"

Eric turns with a Coke in his hand, his face morphing into confusion and then alarm when he sees the tears coursing down my cheeks. The weird thing is I *never* cry. The guys at school call me a sissy and a "whiny little bitch" all the time when they aren't calling me a faggot, but the thing is I never, *never* cry. Normally sadness doesn't reach past my throat. Except suddenly, tonight, I can't stop it.

"Oh," he says. I close my eyes and try to rub the tears

out of them but they keep coming. I feel like a child. "Okay. Okay." I hear footsteps and then Eric's arms are around me, which is surprising. Ever since the kiss we both silently agreed to keep our distance – no more sharing a bed when one of us sleeps over, no more slaps on the shoulder, no more wrestling, and I guess I hadn't noticed how much I missed this. I rest my cheek on his shoulder and decide to stop fighting it. My shoulders shake and I'm distantly aware of the uncontrollable sobs coming out of me, that I'm getting snot and tears all over my friend's nice shirt.

He rubs his hand between my shoulder blades and shushes me, and I hate that under all this pain it feels so good. I want to be friends like we were. I want puberty to never have happened. My mind rushes back to the last time he held me, last year as we sat in the street, and I can't stop imagining that horrible idea: what if I'd been born a real girl, and all of this was different?

Eric sits me down on the couch and I sink into the quicksand cushions. I scramble at his shirt, furrowing my fingers in the cloth like someone holding on for dear life. He stays with me the whole time, whispering against my shoulder.

"Breathe," he says.

I force myself to breathe in through my nose and out through my mouth. My tears dry on my cheeks and soak into Eric's shirt.

In my exhaustion I consider telling him everything that just happened with my dad, with the make-up, with the dumpster. But I can't. I'm headed for a lifetime of repression and pain either way, and it's like Carson always says: if you're going into town, you might as well go in a Lincoln.

Eric squeezes my shoulder. "How can we make you feel better?" he says softly. I rub my eyes and sigh.

"I think I want to try out for the football team," I say, before I really know why I'm saying it.

Eric arches an eyebrow and leans back.

"Wait, what?" he says.

"I know it sounds crazy, but yeah."

And suddenly I *am* sure. I sniffle the last of the mucus away and nod so hard my headache comes back. It's pointless to imagine living in some different reality. I have the life I have. I live where I live. If I can't be a girl then I'll throw myself *completely* into being a boy. "Really?"

"Yeah," I say.

Eric leans down into my field of view and gives me a sceptical look. I shove him away, but with a light touch so he knows I'm only kidding.

"What?" I say. "You think I can't? I seem to remember *you* leaning on *me* back in middle school, and I'm as tall as you now." *That* hurts like hell to think about, but my tear ducts must be spent because I don't start sobbing again. "I'll hit weights with you and Dad and try out before next season. I can do it."

He runs a hand over his scalp and blows out a long breath. "Yeah, sure. But why?"

"Something has to change," I say. It might not be the whole truth but at least it *is* true. "Who I am right now, who I've *been*, it just doesn't work. It has to change."

"But…" Eric rubs a knuckle against his lips and narrows one eye. "*I* like who you are."

He's being generous.

"Thanks," I say, running my fingers through my sweat-matted hair and staring for a while at his shaved hair under the light. "And one other thing."

"Yeah, anything."

"I want you to cut my hair off," I say.

Eric shifts away from me, a shocked look on his face. He takes the ends of my hair between his fingers, pulls the long brown strands towards him. My hair glimmers in the low light of the living room. I haven't cut it since Mom died, but I push that thought away.

"You sure?" Eric asks, incredulous.

"Positive," I reply, suddenly more certain of this choice than anything else I've ever done in my life.

ERIC

I send Morgan to the back porch and run upstairs to Mom's craft room. My parents are away this weekend, at some church couples retreat to work on their marriage, and I have the house to myself. I'm not sure if chopping his hair off will really help – and I have zero clue if him joining the football team will make him feel better – but helping him is the least I can do. Seeing Morgan cry like that, like he used to but worse somehow, more raw and desperate, left me needing to do *something*.

I can tell he's been miserable lately, and maybe that's part of why I've pulled away, and why we've both been bailing on each other, and it's been hard to watch our friendship shift into uncharted territory. I think back to all the times I avoided him, or put space between us because of the kiss, and I feel like an asshole for letting my own muddled worries pull me away when he's clearly needed me more than ever.

I rummage through drawers of beads and ribbons until I finally find a pair of scissors that look big and sharp enough to do the trick. I wonder what he's not telling me, and I start to think maybe a better friend would have figured out what's wrong by now and feel a surge of sour guilt. I'm still mulling everything over when I open the sliding glass door, step onto the back porch, and almost drop my scissors. Morgan's sitting on the rail, shirtless, his eyes hidden in shadow and the strands of his own hair. I suck air through my teeth.

When's the last time I saw him without a shirt? He's so skinny, almost down to the bone, all the muscle from middle school wasted away to nothing. I can count his ribs. I want to toss my scissors aside and hug him again, but then Morgan sees me and pulls his hair back out of his face. Without the hood and his bulky sweatshirt, I realize it's down to his waist. And it's beautiful. Thick like a tangle of branches on a September night, and dark brown, close to black under the porch light.

In a flash I see a hundred memories. His hair blowing in his face, or him dangling from a tree branch and pulling it behind his ear, or him laughing and whipping it carelessly to one side, or…so many other times. I'd never realized it until now. That long hair makes my heart stop.

Standing over Morgan, I don't just want to hug him. I want to kiss him so badly it burns my chest.

"I haven't cut it since Mom died," he says quietly.

"Yeah," I say, my voice catching in my throat.

He scratches his neck and holds up a grey can. "Think your dad'll notice if one of his beers goes missing from the garage fridge?"

I shake my head and he cracks the can, taking a long sip that exposes his slender neck, nearly finishing it in one go. Then he pulls a white plastic chair under the porch light and settles in. His pale skin glows with beaded sweat.

"How short do you want it?"

"All of it," he says. "I want us to match."

I nod silently and begin. I don't want to do this, but I have to.

I have to do it for Morgan.

The scissors flash silver under the light and the night hums with the sounds of summer fading into fall, cicadas and crickets and the occasional car passing by. My street is dark and it feels like we're the only two people in the world right now. We don't talk. I do my best to keep some distance between us, but I still have to brush his cheeks, chin and neck, still have to brace my hand on his shoulder to get the scissors in the best position.

His skin is smooth and surprisingly cool. Wherever our skin connects I feel my own jittery, nervous energy over tonight, and Susan, and my own hair, and everything that's happened between me and Morgan. A spark of electricity passes from me and into him, flooding out of my crowded heart and into his. I wonder what Morgan's heart is like compared to mine. Empty isn't the right word, though it's the first that comes to mind. Minimalist. Maybe it's more like yin and yang, like his heart is a dark, cool room after a hot, exhausting day.

I leave my fingers on his cheek a little longer than I mean to, only to notice that *now* his skin is warm. I look down to find him blushing, his breathing a little heavier. I pull my hand away quickly.

It takes a while and it's nowhere near even, but when I'm finally done Morgan stands up to see his reflection in the sliding glass door. It's not buzzed like mine, more like something you'd see in a movie where a character like Joan of Arc chops all her hair away to join the Crusades, but it's as close to the scalp as I could get. He doesn't smile, but he runs his fingers over his head, squares his shoulders, and nods, satisfied.

I can't shake the feeling that I've hurt him, or that I've destroyed something beautiful. He turns to me and it feels like someone new stands before me. A stranger.

"You like it?" I ask, breaking the silence.

"Yeah," he says, but there's a tightness around his eyes I don't totally trust. "I think Dad has a trimmer I can use, but it's a good start." He kills the last of the beer, throws the can on the ground, and stomps it flat. "Thanks."

We brush all the hair off him and I sweep the porch. The moths silently circle the light above our heads.

After a while Morgan says, "I'm going to get home."

"Right, okay," I reply. I can't help but feel there's a mountain of unsaid words between us.

"Happy birthday," he says.

"You too, man."

I watch Morgan grab his bike and fade off into the darkness, his shorn hair occasionally catching in the shine of a street light. I rub at my own shaved head. As Morgan finally disappears, I find myself kissing my forefinger and middle finger and touching them to the screen door.

"Love you," I whisper. I'm vaguely aware as I mount the stairs that I didn't end the statement with "dude" or "man". When I finally reach my bed it feels large, and cold, and empty. The street lights leave zigzags across my blanket and I'm reminded of the silver flash of scissors and the tumble of Morgan's hair, glimmering as it fell onto the porch.

SIXTEENTH
BIRTHDAY

MORGAN

I hook my right bicep around my left elbow and pull. Warmth spreads through my shoulder and lower back. My body is a machine, and I'm in control. It's hard, and fast, and it does what I tell it, when I tell it. The finger of vodka I mixed into my Gatorade doesn't hurt.

I figured Dad would have noticed the steady dwindle of his supply of alcohol by now, but he does go through a pretty heroic amount himself. I hadn't known that about him – or, well, I knew he drank sometimes, but I never knew how much until I started stealing it from him.

I assume he started after Mom died, which maybe explains a lot about how he's been able to keep up appearances so well, how he's so good at looking the other way. Turns out we both have our secrets. Boys will be boys, right?

But really, if *I* had a "son" who, in the span of a year,

pulled his grades up to a B and went from scrawny, mopey bully-bait to a varsity running back I'd probably look the other way too, to make excuses for the sudden change and what it means. My son drinks? He's sociable. He's being invited to parties. He's gotten in a coupla fights this year? Well, he was smart enough to have them off school grounds.

Dad now seems happy when he's around me. Eric seems happy too. *I'm* not happy, but I'm maybe sort of less miserable. Now I only get punched when I punch first. All in all, this last year's worked out pretty well for everybody.

Almost everybody.

The barbell sits at my feet like an insult. I stretch my other arm. Three hundred and fifty pounds of weight, total, bulges black and rough at its ends. I flex my fingers. The rest of the team has stopped working out and gravitated towards my section of the student weight room. They stand in a semicircle around me with Eric, Nate and Chud in the middle, some muttering to each other, some chanting encouragement, some snickering. The football players think I haven't changed, that I'm still the pussy I was a year ago. They're wrong. I pull my shirt off and crack my neck to drive away the impulse to cover myself back up. I am in control, I tell myself. I take a breath in and the rank BO smell of the weight room invades my nostrils.

A year later. Another birthday. I'm sixteen, and this is

who I am now – more like a man every day. I'd be lying if I said it hasn't been hard. Not the physical training, which was actually pretty easy when you want to hurt yourself all the time, but the first few weeks, when my muscles started showing definition and my shoulders started thickening were…rough.

But then I figured out the trick to living *past* autogynephilia (besides drinking) – you take it a day at a time. Don't think about the past. Don't think about the future. Don't look in mirrors. I'm like the guy from *Memento*, my life a series of disconnected gasps and flashes, no one lasting long enough to hurt for too long.

My film teacher told me he was disappointed in how my interest in film seemed to be fading. He asked if I even wanted to pursue a career in movies any more, which hurt to hear, but then I closed my eyes, walled that moment off from every other moment, and *poof,* it was over. Gone for ever.

A few months ago, Jasmine asked me why I was ignoring her, why I'd changed. Sometimes Jasmine will still catch my eye in the hall and look hurt or, worse, will flip her hair and turn in the opposite direction, and I'll think about how she was the only girl I wanted to be friends with, and now I'm just another asshole high school boy to her. It's agony, but then there's the wall of static again. *Poof.* Gone.

Or, for instance, a Victoria's Secret ad comes on while

I'm hanging out with the guys and they all visibly drool and I realize I'll always be alone in my freakish, desperate yearning to be like what I'm supposed to want, but then… you get the idea. I'm surprised more people haven't figured out this system. Day by day, hour by hour, minute by minute, that's the way to do it. *Poof poof poof.*

"Get on with it, Morgan," Nate says, kicking his sneaker against the weights. "There's only five minutes left of lunch."

"Give him time," Eric says. He scowls at Nate, then smiles at me, and for a moment I hate myself for noticing how he's gotten even more handsome these last few months, how he looks more grown and rugged in a sort of jock-meets-bohemian way, but then I don't think about that because I don't want to. "Go easy. No point doing *this* if you get hurt and can't play tonight."

"It's not like we need him," a senior named Billy-Joe says, under his breath, but I still hear him.

"You *need* somebody to beat your ass," I snap. I take in a sharp breath, squat over the weight, and arch my back. I keep talking without even looking at Billy-Joe. "Maybe you'll finally get a date once your face is rearranged."

"Hot *damn*," Nate says.

"Big talk when we all know you'd be on the bench if your daddy wasn't coach." That's Chud.

I spit on the mat between us and flex my fingers on the barbell. He's too big to take in a fight – two fights so far this season, three over the summer, and one last spring have taught me my limits.

"Go fuck yourself, Chud," I say.

This isn't me, of course. This is just my suit of armour. All I can do is prove myself, now and tonight. If I lift this weight? That's 275 pounds added to my dead lift in less than a year. That's a body honed through *work*, which that sack of meatloaf never had to do. If I contribute to a win tonight? That's our second win against the Pioneers in three years after a fifteen-year losing streak, and there's no coincidence it's me on the team that's made the difference.

I grip. I flex my knees, and they burn like a wildfire. Nothing happens at first. I close my eyes and grind my jaw. My feet shift slightly and I put my back into it. The weight starts to lift and the guys go silent. No more smartass comments now. With shaking knees, I bring my legs, inch by inch, to their full extension. Almost there. None of my muscles want to listen but, and this is the secret, the most *important* secret: I am not my body.

My body is a machine.

Machines don't get to say no. They take orders until they break. I don't care if this machine breaks. I growl and give the order, over and over. And suddenly, though unsurprisingly to me, my back straightens out and my shoulders roll back. The guys start hollering, jumping around, pumping their fists in the air. Their disrespect evaporates like a shallow, scummy puddle.

Three hundred and fifty pounds. Nothing. The barbell drops and the impact rattles the weight room. I slam my chest as the room buzzes around me. Eric runs in and slaps my shoulder, yelling congratulations. I'm an inch taller than him now. I fight my body in that moment – my body that still wants more than a slap on the shoulder – and I win. This machine shuts off when I tell it to. But my heart hurts more than my shoulders or back. I can't look him in the eyes.

"Excited about tonight?" he says. "Birthday blowout!"

"Right, awesome," I reply.

There's a party being thrown by Nate's older brother in Knoxville and we're all carpooling after the game. A *college* party, with college girls. I've had to pretend to be excited for weeks. I try to nonchalantly add, "Is Susan coming?"

It's already hard enough being around them when she invites herself along to hang out with us, her playing with his hair, watching them lace their fingers together, listening to their kissing sounds whenever we go out to a movie.

"No word yet," he says. "She's probably planning some big birthday surprise."

"Girls, right?" I say. What's that even supposed to *mean*? But he laughs anyway, or fakes a laugh. I slap his back with one hand and step away. The bell rings.

"See you tonight," I say. I grab my shirt and head for the door before he can respond.

ERIC

I inhale a protein bar on the way to Advanced English. I've got to keep my energy levels up before the big game tonight. The room's empty when I get there, nobody but me in a hurry to discuss ancient Greek poetry. Gives me a quiet moment to skim back through the assigned passages from *The Odyssey,* and I focus on the section we're reading today, about Tiresias in the underworld.

"Know why I like you?" Susan says.

I blink and look up from my book to find her leaning over me. She smiles, flips her hair, and sits on my desk. I focus on my beautiful girlfriend and all the details of her I'm still learning, like the pattern of the freckles on her shoulders, and can't think of much to say. My family might be coming apart at the seams and Morgan might be turning into someone I barely recognize, but at least *this* part of my life is still here, uncomplicated and good.

Susan's finger tips up my chin.

"Why's that?" I say.

"Are you a jock? Are you a nerd? Are you a hipster?" She shrugs. "It's the *layers*."

"I try," I say.

"So I wanted to talk to you about your birthday present…" She leans in for a kiss as the rest of the class files in. Sometimes I kind of suspect Susan likes me more for *what* I am than *who* I am, like it's important for her to be seen with me. But I genuinely like being around her, so I move my lips against hers and let the thought fly away.

"Save it for the backseat," my English teacher, Mrs Brown, says. A few of the students give a scandalized, "Ohhhhhhhh." Susan's face turns red, but when she drops into her own seat I notice she's smiling.

Class proceeds. As interested as I am, it *is* the golden hour after lunch, so it's hard not to drift off.

My phone buzzes in my pocket and I flinch in surprise. The students around me quietly laugh. Susan hisses and I pull my phone out, opening a text from her. I glance at it, and immediately feel my cheeks turn hot.

I think I'm ready, it reads. *Tonight?* A line of hearts and suggestive smiley faces line the bottom of the message. We've talked about *it* before, but I didn't want to push. I grin to myself and send back a smiley face. If Susan is ready then I'm ready too.

We could probably go to my house, as long as my

parents aren't whisper-fighting in their room – which is pretty much the norm these days. With both Isaac and Peyton permanently moved out now, maybe it feels like they have less to hide, or maybe things have just gotten *that* bad. Isaac's all the way in Seattle, drafted by the Seahawks, and nobody's heard anything from Peyton in for ever – I can't believe it, but I miss him. It would be nice to have someone at home to distract from Mom and Dad's constant sniping.

My brain fast-forwards to after tonight's game, to how it will all go down, when I stop in my tracks, remembering that it would mean bailing on the college party and Morgan and my birthday plans – loose as they are. Barring the third grade chicken pox fiasco, our birthday streak still stands, and it seems like a shame to break it. But, I mean, I can't tell Susan that. What guy refuses to lose their virginity so he can hang with his friend?

I'd be lying if I said a small part of me doesn't want to prove, to myself if nobody else, that I really am straight. The kiss doesn't haunt me as much now that Morgan's gone full diesel – not a glimmer of attraction since he shaved his head and started putting on muscle – so I figure it really was just how feminine he used to be, but it's still hard not to shake sometimes that my first kiss was with a boy. I don't know. It's nice not dealing with the confusion as much, but sometimes I miss the way things were, confusion and all. But I tell myself that Morgan doesn't seem to want to go back. He's happy now, right? All I want is for Morgan to be happy.

That afternoon, I try to find Morgan to explain. His afternoon history class is in the room next to the chemistry lab. I wait by the door, but when the last student files out with no sign of him, I frown. Where the hell is he? I can't text him in the halls without having my phone taken away, so I sigh and make my way to German, my last class of the day, resigning myself to being late as the second bell rings. I'm practically running when I pass by the back loading bay, near the cafeteria, hear a door creak, and look up to find Morgan slipping in through the doors.

"There you are," I say. "What were you doing?"

Morgan blinks slowly as if he just woke up from a nap. He shoves his hands in his pockets and shrugs.

"I was tired from the weight room," he says. His voice is distant. "Needed some air."

Something sharp hits my nose and I realize it's the smell of vodka. Most of the guys on the team drink on weekends. It's a lot of stress to have a whole town putting their hopes on you every week, especially in a town like this, where athletic scholarships are the only way out for a lot of us.

More and more, though, I've noticed Morgan doesn't *just* drink on the weekends. At first he would show up to parties with a bottle of rum and mix it with soda, and that was all right. Then he started leaving the liquor at home and showing up to parties with his eyes already glassy and distant. Now, if I'm being honest, that's how he looks a lot.

"Okay," I say. "Anyway. I have to cancel our plans tonight."

"That's fine," Morgan says, not even a lick of curiosity in his voice.

"You're sure?" I'd rehearsed this in my head and it's not going the way I expected. Like it's our birthday and it stings that he truly doesn't care, but I guess *I'm* the one cancelling.

"It is?"

"Yeah, it's cool."

"'Cause Susan said she's ready to—" I start to say, but he just sucks something out of his teeth.

"Yeah," he says. We reach his destination and he turns for the door. "Do your thing."

"We can reschedule."

"If you want," he says. "I'll see you at the game." He gives me a perfunctory wave and slips into his class.

I stand in the empty hallway, clenching and unclenching my fists, not completely sure what just happened.

MORGAN

My body isn't *just* a machine.

It's a well-oiled machine. A high-octane machine. A *killing* machine. The first half of the game, when I was on the bench because Dad didn't want to seem like he was playing favourites, was bad. *Shameful.* The Pioneers rinsed us. We were down by three touchdowns, Nate and a freshman on the bench with a wrenched ankle and a possibly broken finger. Halftime came and went. Dad gave me the signal. I popped my knuckles.

I'm no good on defence, just not big enough yet, but that's fine because you don't come back from a showing like this with defence. I catch a punt and make it within spitting distance of the Pioneers' end zone, gritting my teeth so hard they might break. I ram and twist through guys trying to grab me, to throw me down. I make myself a threat with each play, and when I slip through their line and barrel forwards to the left, they're so focused on me, on trying to pull me to the ground, they barely notice as the pass goes to Eric and we score.

The crowd screams, finally given hope for the first time in this embarrassment of a game, and it feels good – not as good, say, as the dreams where I'm a cheerleader, where I'm a girl in the bleachers watching her boyfriend, where I'm on the girls' basketball or volleyball teams, where I'm a cool rebel like Jasmine smoking under the bleachers and rolling her eyes at all of this. No, this feels good like winning at a video game feels good. A number gets bigger, and I'll be rewarded for it, and that's that. No euphoric high means no crash when reality hits.

We plod on and start to turn the game around. It isn't even hard. I yank helmets when refs aren't looking. I kick shins and spit on jerseys. The thing is, it's a head game. The more they hate me, the more they'll run after me when a play starts, even if they *know* the ball's going to Eric. And if I'm being honest, I already hate myself, so I'm basically an expert in how to hate me.

I eat dirt a few times, but it's not like I haven't gotten my ass kicked before, and at least now I've got a helmet, and the adults will step in if things get out of hand. Where were the adults before? How many of them stood up for me when people knocked things out of my hands, punched me in the stomach, spat on me, called me a faggot? And now they're cheering? I don't know who's more of a hypocrite – me or them.

Long live football.

One of the Pioneers' defensive line spears me on the next play, flinging me to the ground like a rag doll, and the rattling impact manages to knock an unwelcome memory out from behind the static.

It's the first Christmas break after Mom died, and Eric's visiting his grandma for two weeks, leaving me with nothing to do but stay at home with a grief-ridden Dad or wander Thebes on my bike. It's late in the day, the sun beginning to set. I park my bike by the coffee shop, hoping to buy a hot chocolate with the crumpled bills in my pocket so I can sit outside and watch the blinking lights strung up and down Main Street. But when I get in line I hear snickering. I ignore it. Little pieces of paper and trash strike the back of my neck and my old, oversized coat swallowing up my tiny body. I ignore that too. Then voices shaking with laughter call my name and, even though I shouldn't, I turn. Three boys I vaguely recognized from the junior varsity team, probably sophomores, huge compared to me, smirk at me from a corner table.

"What?" I say.

"Told you," one of the boys, I think his name was Clark, says. He leans over and playfully punches another boy (Peter maybe?) in the arm. "Told you it was him."

"What do you want?" I say.

"God," Peter says, "what's up your ass? Ever heard of Christmas spirit?"

"You threw trash at me," I say.

"'You thwew twash at me,'" says a third boy, the largest of them, named Zack. "Don't be a baby."

"What do you want?" I look around to see if any of the adults plan to step in. Either none of them have noticed, which isn't likely considering how loud these three are, or they think the Wildcats are untouchable.

"We just had a question," Clark says.

"Yeah," Peter adds.

"*What?*" I say, hating how my voice shakes.

"Why'd you quit youth league?" Zack says. His face splits into a grin. Before I can answer he continues. "We heard you were *real* popular in the locker room and you got bored once you'd sucked everybody off."

I don't know what that *means* but I get the gist. I know what they're calling me, and I let my shame and anger push me past thinking.

"My mom died," I say, and *god* it hurt so much to say it, but I hope it'll make them leave me alone.

"Bet she killed herself," Peter says.

My feet carry me towards their table. I snatch one of their mugs. They're too busy laughing and elbowing each other to notice.

"I'd off myself too if my son was a f—" Clark begins, but then I tip the mug and pour coffee all over their books and laps. "What the fuck? Little psycho!"

"Hey!" a booming, matronly voice calls. We all freeze

and I turn to see the owner, a stocky white-haired woman in a stained apron, rounding the counter with her hands on her hips. I scan the coffee shop and realize I know almost everyone there – teachers, other students' parents, older kids from high school. All of them watch us with wide eyes, whispering. I let out a sigh of relief through the rage and shame, because *now* at least adults are paying attention. They *have* to do something. The woman stops near me, looming over me, and scowls. "You have to leave."

It doesn't register for a moment. I turn to the boys, feeling *so* smug, because obviously she means them, but then my body goes numb as reality sets in.

"Me?" I say.

"Yeah, you," she says. "You can't pull that kind of thing in here."

"But they—" I said.

"Don't care," she says, her hands up. "Doesn't matter."

This is when I start wearing hoodies all the time – at first just to hide the bruises they gave me later in the park and then, I guess, to hide from myself. Dad and Eric never find out.

The memory pulls at me like hands rising from a midnight grave in a bad horror movie. I kick it away and play through the pain. It's better to use it than to let it use me, so I pretend every Pioneer across the line of scrimmage is one of those three older boys.

We crawl our way back, never letting them play offence

186

for more than a couple yards. It's a slaughter, a red tide flowing past our ankles. I look up and five seconds are left on the clock, with them only ahead by a desperate field goal, and us ten yards away. I see fear in their eyes and realize it's all been worth it just to see an opponent go pale and back away from me when I twitch at them.

The quarterback calls hike. Eric runs downfield. I break to the side. More of the opposition follow me than him. Great. But then I look back and see two of them break our line and rush for the quarterback. Even if I can't see his face I read panic in his movements.

Things go slow. I'm so close to him that we make eye contact, and I can tell he wants to toss the ball off and pivot this into a running play. I shake my head desperately. He's got two wide receivers, if he'd just keep his head and throw the ball.

Please don't toss it to me. *Please* stick to the play.

He lobs it, underhand, in my direction. Pioneers pile onto him like an avalanche, but all I can see is the ball. I grab it and turn, still holding onto a glimmer of hope, only to see four Pioneers hurtling towards me. For a minute I let myself believe there's a gap my smaller body can shoot through, even take a couple strides towards it, but if it was ever there it snaps shut.

My only option is to run to the side and hope I'm fast enough to juke back towards the end zone before I step out of bounds. For the first time in a long time panic melts the barrier between my body and myself and I'm whole again, a desperate animal scrambling. I pump my legs, scream wordlessly, try to will the defenders away from me. And when I turn, my toes just grazing the OB line, I think I might have made it.

But then two hundred pounds of angry teenage boy spears me in the side and I'm driven to the dirt. The clock ticks down. The game ends. They win.

Their side cheers, and I feel someone kick me in the side. It feels like every other time I've been kicked while I was down. Nothing's changed.

I don't really register things for a while. There's a red haze, a pulsing in the glands at my throat, a tightness in the back of my skull. There are flashes as I stand, cross the field, stumble into the locker room. I stand there for a moment, teeth grinding, breath coming in deep gulps. The locker room hums with an industrial fan and the distant, profane sound of cheering. Two ideas tear at each other in my head like caged, hungry tigers.

Idea one: souls are real, or boy and girl brains are real, and I am a girl with shitty enough luck to have been born in a boy's body, and now that I've *really* given this the old college try, it's clear I never had any choices from the start.

Idea two: I'm a pathetic, self-pitying pervert who couldn't even do *this* right.

I crouch, cover my ears, and close my eyes. A sound erupts from me and the groan crescendos into a scream.

I stand, crank my arm back, and whip my helmet through the air. It slams into a locker and bounces away, leaving a dent, the bars over the face warped and broken. I don't feel *good*, but I feel *better*, so I decide to cut loose.

I kick over benches and tear down posters. My fist clips a locker and the pain blooms crimson, pushing away every other feeling, so I punch it on purpose and feel even better. I punch, and punch, and punch, ignoring as my hand first goes numb and then begins to glow with pain. All I see are the dents I make in the metal and the red smears I leave.

"Morgan!" Dad says.

I don't stop. The door busts off its hinges and bends out from the lock but I keep going, punching the wall behind it, happy to be a feral animal because it's a reprieve from being me. Anything would be better than being me, because *what has all of this been for*? I have slowly strangled the real me with all of this – with alcohol, and weights, and football. The locker room talk, the stupid score, the endless, mindless strategies. And for what? *For what?*

Someone grabs me around the waist and throws me to the ground. I look up, panting and dazed, to see Eric staring down at me, still in his pads, his hair plastered to his head. He's saying something, but there's a ringing in my ears and I can't catch my breath. For a moment I'm ashamed for him to see me like this, ashamed that even when I'm trying to be normal I can't be normal, but then another plume of rage rises up from somewhere deep.

He reaches down to help me up and I slap his hand away.

In this moment, I *hate* him for being a part of my life. Him *and* Dad – if I didn't love them, if I didn't care what they thought about me, if I weren't so desperately afraid of losing them, I'd be that much closer to freedom. I wish they would disappear.

I wish I would disappear.

Dad leans into my field of vision. "Clear out for a minute, boys," he says. He pulls me up and helps me to a bench, wraps an arm around my shoulder. I don't fight him. In a fuzzy post-rage way, I think about how much more he's hugged me this last year. Why didn't he hug me before? I'm sure in my right mind I could come up with a dozen excuses, but why should I? Or maybe *this* is my right mind, finally, and the truth is this: for him, just like for every other guy in this dying, dilapidated, dogshit town, whatever's wrong with me is catching, and he wasn't even willing to risk it for his own child.

We sit there, shoulders touching for a while. He doesn't say anything yet. My breath steadies.

"You're taking this pretty hard, yeah?" he finally says.

"I guess."

"Let you in on a little secret?" I don't respond. "It's just a game."

"You know it isn't," I say. "It's *everything* at this school." I swallow and raw pain needles at my throat.

"Listen. Just because something's serious doesn't mean

you have to *take* it seriously. I know you're passionate, and I'm *glad* you're passionate, but…it's also supposed to be fun."

I shrug.

"How about we head into Knoxville next weekend?" he says. "Just you and me, a guys' weekend. We'll catch a Vols game and just relax, remind you why you liked football in the first place."

I shrug again, lighter this time. The more the rage fades, the more confused I feel. Everything bleeds out into the same uniform grey.

"And listen," he says, and rubs my arm. "I'm being serious here. You should be *proud*. You've done so well. Helped get us *this* close to making history after, what, five years off the field? You're a goddamn *prodigy*, Morgan. And there's always next year, right? We'll get 'em next year."

Next year. I blink. My eyes feel dry. *Next* year. I make the mistake of thinking about the future in a moment when the veil is down, when I'm weak and can't force dangerous thoughts to go somewhere else. I imagine keeping this up for another year. I imagine graduating high school like this, going to college like this. I imagine my body hairy. My muscles thick. Then more time passes. Legs get skinny, belly pooches out, hair recedes at the temple, beard grows in and turns grey. I imagine marrying a woman I don't like so I don't feel guilty when she realizes

I can't love her. I try imagining past thirty and it's just a wall of static. I might as well be dead.

It's easy to hold your breath when the surface is right there, and I realize that's what I've been doing. Except now that I'm paying attention, it turns out the surface isn't there. I'm *miles* down, so deep light can't reach, so deep the pressure's crushing my ribcage, and if I try to swim up, my body will twist into something unrecognizable.

What do you do when you can't swim up, you can't swim down, and staying put will suffocate you? Where is my help? Why hasn't anybody realized I need *help*?

Help is never coming, I realize. It never was.

"Yeah," I say. I nod like a machine and stand to leave. He gives me a hopeful smile and I blink. "Yeah. Sorry. Good talk."

I grab my backpack and stride through the locker room doors into the cool wetness of the field, and find Eric nearby, pale and biting his nails. When he notices me he jogs over, almost like he wants to hug me, but then stops short.

"Hey," he says. "We were worried about you."

"Who's we?" I demand. I sidestep him and peer out towards the field and the bleachers. The idea that people are talking about me behind my back makes my blood boil. That they think I'm weak.

"Me, William, the other guys…"

I try to shove past Eric again.

192

"What?" Eric grabs my shoulder and turns me so I'm looking at him. "Morgan. Hey."

"*William*," I say. The game loss was the quarterback's fault. William. Freshman. Junior varsity. He was only on the field because Nate got hurt. He shouldn't have been on the field at *all*, because he clearly hasn't paid attention to a word Dad said to him. It's *his* fault I feel this way. It's *his* fucking fault.

I'm going to start a fight with William. It feels like every cell in my body is trying to pull itself apart, like my being wants nothing more than to melt into a sewer drain, and hurting and being hurt is the only way to hold myself together.

"I think we should go somewhere quiet," Eric says. "You clearly need to talk. I can cancel my plans with Susan—"

"Oh, no," I say. "I'm fine." I wipe blood on my jersey and sniff. "Just do me a favour and tell me where William went, then feel free to go fuck your cheerleader."

"What the *fuck*, dude?" Eric says. He takes a step back and looks at me like I'm a car accident. "Why are you acting like this?"

"Acting like what? I just want to know where William is."

"And *I'm* trying to help y—"

"You can't!" I hiss. I grab his jersey and pull him in so his face is inches from mine, and as much as my heart aches remembering the last time we were this close, my gut screams to push him away again. "I can't be helped. Okay? Drop it and then leave me the *fuck* alone."

"Morgan," he says, a pathetic, whiny edge in his voice. What the fuck does *he* have to whine about? He has *everything*: his family has money, he's socially well-adjusted, he's dating one of the prettiest girls in school, his parents are alive, his future's bright. I'm probably the only dark spot in his whole life. "Dude, please, you're my best—"

I push him away again and scowl. "Does Susan know she wasn't your first kiss?"

"Wh-what?"

"Did. You. Tell. Your. Girlfriend. You. Kissed. Me?"

"No," he says, his voice suddenly small. He rubs his arm and looks down at the grass. "I didn't. I didn't want to—"

"*I'll* tell her," I say. His eyes go wide and his gaze snaps back to mine. His mouth pulls into a thin, panicked line. "I'll tell *everyone*, unless *you* tell *me* where William went."

He stares at me for a long time, flexing and unflexing his fingers while we listen to the murmur of the receding crowd and the distant crunch of tyres on gravel. His nostrils flare and his panic shifts into a deep frown.

"The parking lot," Eric says. His voice is as flat and grey as cement. "They're all hanging out by Nate's car, waiting for you."

"See?" I say. "That was easy!"

"What're you gonna do?"

"He cost us the game," I say. Who *actually* cares about the game? Not me. Not now, not any more, not really. The truth is I just need to feel anything but what I'm feeling right now. I'm a cornered animal and it's time to bite. "I'm gonna fucking kill him."

"Morgan," Eric says. "What…come *on*, dude, this isn't you. Let's just go talk."

"Get out of my face, Eric."

"Fine," Eric says. "Have it your way."

I turn and march towards the parking lot. Part of me, a little voice like something out of one of those stupid dreams, begs me to stop, to turn, to at least look over my shoulder and see if Eric's still there. I stuff the voice down into the void.

The parking lot's half empty at this point, and the guys are easy enough to find near the back, huddled around Nate's car, talking and laughing even though we lost. How nice for them. Nate notices me first, shooting one arm into the air and whistling.

"Took you long enough!" he calls. "You done with the locker room, drama queen? The rest of us need to change."

"Yeah," I say. "Have at it."

The team flows around me in the opposite direction, some of them still in their pads, some shirtless with their jerseys over their shoulders and their gear hanging loose in thick fingers. I notice William among them, looking at me with the same pathetic worry that makes me want to destroy him. I grab his elbow with my good hand.

"Hey!" he says. William jerks his arm, but I squeeze harder. "Can I *help* you?"

Some of the guys keep going. Some pause in this little island of light and watch, though even they keep their distance. I stare William down, watching as his face shifts from confusion to frustration to indignation. Then I take all the pain in my heart, all the screaming noise in my head, and squeeze it down into a white-hot point of light. With one step forward, almost chest to chest with this kid who never *really* did anything to wrong me, I lean my head back, and crash my forehead into his.

ERIC

Once Morgan's around the bleachers and out of sight, I take a different route to the back lot behind the music building, feeling with every step like I'm floating one foot behind myself. Even without the threat, I've got no interest in watching him destroy himself.

Morgan wouldn't actually tell Susan, would he? He wouldn't tell *everyone*? These questions cycle out of control for most of the walk, but as I reach my car, formerly Peyton's and Isaac's before that, I realize the answers are yes and yes.

He's sick. I don't know *how*, I'm not a therapist, but something went wrong in his head years ago. He needs help. I try not to think about it, I *want* to say it's not my problem. But...when you've known someone this long, they become your problem. What if I'd told him not to try out for the football team? What if I'd refused to shave his head? What if I hadn't helped him get in shape so fast? What if, what if, what if…?

I want my friend back, is the thing. Under all the specifics is that single, simple, thought: *My friend is gone and I want him back.*

The idea that I've lost him for ever slides through my brain like a cold knife. My eyes burn and my vision blurs. I pull over to the side of the road, wondering for a minute if I'm allergic to something or if I'm sick, only to touch my cheek and realize I'm crying. How long's it been since I last cried? I don't even remember. Knowing what all my friends would say if they saw me like this adds one more crack to the foundation.

Nothing to do but get it out of my system before Susan sees, so I put in a sad mix I burned to CD, rest my forehead on the steering wheel, and hope it passes. I'm out of practice with crying, and a little embarrassed, but in a way it feels nice letting it out. Or it's bad and nice at the same time – like exercise.

A new track fades from the background, pushing its lyrics into my brain.

"Pale Blue Eyes" by The Velvet Underground. The guitar bubbles like a stream on a fall day. The singer almost whispers.

I remember that afternoon when Morgan fell from the tree, when I *first* noticed that he was beautiful. It feels so sad to think that in the past tense. I remember crouching over him and his eyes opening wide and really *seeing* them for the first time, not pale blue but greenish blue, and he looked up at me with so much relief and affection as I pulled him to his feet that I froze.

Now his eyes are hard and dim.

But I can't wallow like this for ever. Maybe my memory's faulty, but it occurs to me that anyone who saw the whole span of our lives could never accuse me of not doing my best. Maybe my best wasn't good enough, but that's not my fault. All I can do is keep going, right? Maybe you can't fix other people. Maybe we never were going to be friends for ever. After a few last long, shuddering breaths I'm back to normal, on the road, barrelling towards some kind of manhood.

MORGAN

It occurs to me, as William grabs my busted wrist and wrenches it to the side, that of our two positions, quarterback is a lot less cardio-intensive, so he's nowhere near as tired as me. He punches me with his free hand over and over, my vision flashing black and white. And, you know, he's got the two good hands because he didn't punch a locker.

I kick at his legs but he shoves me back and, vision swimming, I trip over my ankles and fall to the pavement. Really, if I'd wanted to *win* this would have been a stupid idea. He jumps on me, straddling my hips, and starts punching again, wildly, body blows and hits to the face alike. The pads absorb some, but they don't protect my stomach. Eventually, after a sort of adrenaline eternity, the guys watching must decide I've had enough. They approach carefully and grab William under the arms. He fights them at first, desperate in his fury to keep laying hands on me, but finally relents. They bring him to his feet, and just when I think I can start breathing again, his face shifts into one last rictus and he kicks me three sharp times in my already aching leg.

"*Fucker!*" he says as they drag him away. He wipes blood from his nose and spits as close to me as he can get. "Fucking *psycho*! Maybe you woulda made the run if you weren't always *drunk*."

Yeah, I think. *Maybe. Probably.*

They fade away from the overhead lights, presumably returning to the locker room. Nobody stays behind to make sure I'm okay. Fair enough. I lie like that for a while, letting the lights spin above me.

After I lose count of the minutes I slowly sit up, shivering at the pain in my stomach and back, the world blurry through my quickly swelling right eye. Once that's accomplished, I get my legs under me, wince when I put too much weight on my hurt ankle, shift a little, and stand on wobbling legs. Progress. My stomach starts to rebel, but I clamp down on it as I sling my backpack around, fish around in the disorganized mess of papers inside, and eventually find my cell phone. *Why* do I want my cell phone? I hold it out, reeling, and realize I was operating on autopilot for a minute there.

I guess my instinct was to call Eric. My stomach voices its displeasure even more at that. Now that I've purged my system with adrenaline and pain, I feel pretty clear-headed and rational, at least compared to a few minutes ago. The things I said to him are actually starting to sink in. I was cruel to him, and what if that was the last straw? What if he doesn't want to see me again?

My hand starts shaking. I *have* to apologize. I start dialling his number, trying to think of what to say that could possibly make this better, but the point is moot since the call goes to voicemail. He probably screened it because he's mad at me.

Except I know what he's doing tonight. I picture my name glowing on his cell as it vibrates pathetically on his night stand. Either way I feel more alone in the universe than I ever have. I notice the voice message is still recording and suddenly it's all too much to bear. I drop my phone on the concrete, raise my good foot, and stamp it until the screen goes dark.

ERIC

Susan presses her face into my shoulder and lets out a soft, muffled giggle as I unlock my front door, filling my body with warmth, most of the night's stress and shame happily melting away with the smell of lavender and mango. I'd picked her up at her house, all smiles and bouncy ponytail. We drove back to mine, noticing both my parents' cars are still gone from the driveway.

"Is anybody home?" Susan whispers so loud I'm sure the neighbours can hear her.

"Nope," I say as we step inside. Dad was at the game, and then went out drinking with his work buddies. Mom is at one of her book clubs, which really just means she's drinking white wine with her friends.

My girlfriend throws herself over the couch with a happy squeal and kicks her legs, then fixes me with a half-lidded, flirtatious gaze.

"Well then," she says as she slithers off the back of the couch and leans against the arm, her eyes glittering. "How about I give you your present right here, right now?"

I sit on the arm of the couch, cup my hand around the back of her neck, and kiss her deeper than it feels like I ever have, trying to transform all my sadness from watching Morgan break down into something else. This can be something else, I tell myself. "Let's go upstairs."

Once we're in my bedroom, Susan shoves me lightly and I fall back on the bed, where she crawls up and hovers above me, her face a silhouette against the lamp above. Then she climbs on top of me, slowly unbuttons her shirt, and casts it aside.

We're really doing this. Okay. *Okay.*

My mind buzzes, every other thought I've ever had in my life cast aside. My body feels like it's on fire. I want this, and I can tell Susan wants this too.

"Go slow," she whispers, and all I can do is nod.

It feels like a blast furnace in my room. I wipe sweat from my face and rub the back of her neck.

"I need water," she says as she rolls to the side. "Could you be the best boyfriend on earth and get me a glass of water?"

"Your wish is my command," I say. I slip on my boxers and head to the kitchen. My heart is still pounding and I can't help but think *that* was amazing. When I return, I find Susan sitting cross-legged on my bed, my guitar across her lap, strumming at the strings.

"You never play any more," she says. "How come?"

"I dunno. I guess I grew out of it." I take the guitar from her and it's dusty from being stuck in a corner for at least a year. I palm a few chords and hum, the pleasure of playing coming back to me.

"That sounds good," she says, her eyes hooded. "You look good too."

I feel my cheeks turn red and smile sheepishly. She reaches out her hand and I take it, placing the guitar against my bed. Susan curls into me, lying down and pulling my hand across her chest, her head facing the window. I join her and we lie in silence, her back pressed against my stomach, just listening to the sound of our breathing as we drift to sleep.

I'm almost completely unconscious when I hear my phone buzz on my night stand. I grab it and see a text from Mom and, further back, a missed call from Morgan with a minute-long voicemail. My phone must have been under the blankets or something, because I wouldn't have screened him. I listen to the message, but it's just static rustling that ends in a sickening crunch— *What the hell?*

I listen to it again, trying to get a sense of what happened to Morgan, why he called in the first place.

Anyone else might think this was a butt dial. But it feels weird. Wrong.

Susan's asleep on my arm, so I use one hand to text him back. *You good?*

Ten minutes later and there's no response. I try calling him and the phone goes straight to voicemail. I watch the ceiling fan go around and around. Counting the minutes. I call again. Still no answer. That old, ominous pressure crawls up the back of my neck, like every nerve ending in my body is banging at the door to my head, demanding that I pay attention.

Susan rolls over and looks at me, her eyebrows quickly coming together in sleepy concern. "What's up?" she asks.

I pause, unsure what to say. "I think there's something wrong with Morgan."

MORGAN

One of my teeth feels loose. I feel my face to see if something's wrong. My hand comes away streaked with red. There's rum and gin at home under Dad's bed. That'll help.

Riding my bike home feels like an eternity of pressure on my busted ankle. What's left of Main Street streaks by in the night, looking like nothing so much as a succession of desiccated, moonlit corpses. I pass the porches of shotgun houses, where starkly lit clusters of friends lounge with cigarettes and beers, smoke mingling with the cloud of insects above them. All chatter stops as I pass and I imagine how I must look in my torn, bloodstained jersey, my face probably fucked seven ways to Sunday: like some kind of sad, desperate cryptid, the Thebes Ghoul limping out of the darkness on its way from one failure to the next.

Eventually, after I'm not sure how long, I reach our trailer, mount the steps, and unlock the door to the living room. Dad's still at school, going over tonight's game with the assistant coaches. I flip the lights on to our normal tableau of piles of laundry and unwashed dishes.

Slam the door. Crouch. Squeeze my head. Breathe roughly through clenched teeth as, now that I'm alone again with nothing to do, the unbound memories and unwanted thoughts come flooding back. I look down and find a yellow envelope on the floor, corners faded, familiar looping handwriting punching my chest harder than even William could.

Morgan, Sixteen.

Breathe. Breathe. Breathe.

I pick up the letter, stand on throbbing knees, and toss it on the coffee table. Not yet, can't read it yet.

I limp into Dad's darkened room and chew my cheeks hard enough to draw blood. The liquor's under the bed where it always is. I leave the rum by Mom's letter and take the gin out to the front steps. I start to drink. Time slurs like a truck on black ice.

It doesn't start as a plan. It just starts as never-ending pain and my brain's a beehive, but then I lift the bottle for another pull, and it's empty, and I realize...well, a human liver can only take so much. When I blink my eyes don't exactly match up. A liver can only take so much I think again, and *my body needs a liver to stay alive* and fuck

I don't want to be alive.

That's the solution. What do you do when you're stuck underwater and you can't swim up or down? You relax and you take a big, watery breath.

God, why'd I never think of this before? I've thought of not wanting to be alive, but never in an actionable way. I throw the empty gin bottle into the gravel driveway and watch it shatter with vague disinterest, rage and a loneliness so deep it screams.

Mom's letter calls at me from inside the house. If I make it to heaven after this, and see Mom again, will she be mad at me? Can feelings get hurt in heaven?

I head inside, flop on the couch while reaching for the rum, and dig my thumbnail under the envelope's seal. I bet feelings *do* get hurt in heaven, just not much. Like a skinned knee for your heart. I slide the letter out, but I don't unfold it yet.

Maybe I'll be a woman in heaven. Not the first time I've thought *that*, not by a mile, but it occurs to me maybe there are no women and no men there, or maybe the desire to be someone different will get burned out of me on the way up. Or maybe I'll go to hell.

I unfold the letter, flick on the side lamp, and read. My vision blurs. I close one eye and try to focus. Mom's handwriting is shakier and fainter than before, like she barely has the strength to go on.

Morgan,

Sixteen years old. What a milestone. This is where things will really start to open up for you, son. More and more you're going to be independent. I worry to think about it even now, with you watching cartoons in your pyjamas in the other room. But I worried when you learned to walk too. That had to happen, and this has to happen. God. I worry, but I wish I could see it.

Anyway. I've said all this before. You know I love you. You know I miss you and I don't want to leave you. I don't want to miss your sixteenth birthday. So here's your present: I don't know what your father said in order to leave you alone tonight, but he's in on my secret. He's headed to Nashville to pick up my old car from your grandma, where it's waited for you this whole time. He'll be back with it in the morning and you'll go together to register it in your name. Surprise! Drive carefully.

I wish I could see you behind the wheel, a girlfriend tucked under your arm, the man you're becoming. I wish I was there to see you all grown up. No longer just my little boy.

Happy birthday, baby. I love you.
Mom

I finish the letter and I'm in the hall on the floor, curled around my aching, twisting stomach, sobbing so hard I can't breathe, my mangled hand over my eyes while I bite down on the knuckles of my left hand.

Things slip out of focus again. There are broken dishes at my feet and I'm sitting in the kitchen, sniffling uncontrollably as I chug cheap cooking wine. Black. White. Points of light floating in and out.

I'm in the bathroom, pills falling through my fingers like sand. What are these? Hard to say, really. I swallow as many as I can. I fall against the tub and hold an empty bottle to my cheek, revelling in the cool feel of the glass, in this last minor comfort. It's hard to hold onto a thought. Things come and go in flashes.

The last thing I know before things go completely black is that I'm above the toilet, mouth hanging open in a wordless sob, vaguely aware that there's more red in the bowl than there should be. And I think, with startling clarity given the circumstances: *At least I did this right.*

ERIC

It feels like there's something at the back of my throat, something pulling at my ribs like a fish hook. I can't even name it, but I *have* to see Morgan right now. I *have* to.

Every moment we're on the road I half expect wailing sirens and red, strobing lights to whip by on their way to his trailer park. But it's insane, right? I drive exactly five miles over the speed limit, and I talk like everything's normal, and I hope Susan doesn't notice how white my knuckles are.

I drop off Susan at her house, giving her a kiss and a million apologies, then race towards Morgan's. I turn into his trailer park like a stunt driver, kicking a spray of gravel into the front office before speeding through its familiar lanes. When I reach his trailer I don't even park, just roll to a stop with two tyres in the grass and jump out.

The lights are on. That's good. I head for the door, but

a sharp crunching sound under my shoes draws my attention. I look down to find a torn gin label and shattered glass strewn across the driveway. I feel planted in place, like in a nightmare where no matter how fast you run or how hard you hit it's never good enough, but this is *real*. I walk through the fear like so many spiderwebs and don't even knock, just test the front door, find it unlocked, and push it open.

"Morgan?" I step inside. Hard to tell if anything's out of place with how messy their trailer usually is, but there's an envelope and a letter on the couch.

"Hey, Morgan?"

A groan drifts from the hallway. I run down the hall and skid to a stop when I reach the bathroom door and the acid smell of vomit hits my nose. My heart stops when I turn and see Morgan, my oldest friend, the person I love maybe the most in the world, sprawled on the floor, face down in blood and puke.

"Morgan!"

I grab a towel, turn him over, and do my best to wipe the filth from his face and neck. It's matted in his hair, on his jersey. There are pills strewn *everywhere*. Tylenol, ibuprofen, *melatonin* of all things, old antibiotics.

His left eyebrow is split wide open and his nose is clearly broken, twin lines of smeared red and brown painting everything from his lips down to his chin, like he hit his face on the bathtub. His eyes flutter, open a fraction of an inch, and then close again. I look around, desperately trying to think if any medicine they might have in the trailer can help, or to figure out what's wrong in the first place, or *something*, and notice another empty liquor bottle discarded near the tub.

How much did he *drink*? And with all these pills? Was he trying to…?

Oh. Oh god. He *was*. One of the last things he said to me bursts up from the darkness: "I can't *be* helped."

I look Morgan over and realize that under the blood and puke he's tinged blue everywhere, especially his nose and the ends of his fingers. I shake him and scream his name and his eyes don't open again.

"Come *on*, Morgan," I say. My voice shakes like a tin roof in a thunderstorm. "Come on!" A surge of anger rises up my throat. I shake him harder. "You can't do this to me. Wake up!"

He doesn't answer. I beat his chest and wipe my eyes, only distantly aware of how dirty I'm getting. My breath comes in gasps.

"Morgan, listen to me. I'm here. I got you." My breathing is raspy and I choke on my words. "Please. I need you." Morgan says nothing and I realize what I have to do.

I stand, wipe my hands clean, and call 911.

MORGAN

My brain is a minefield of agony. I turn, tugging covers around myself, and feel a sharp pull at the inside of my elbow. It's real pain, and I realize with dread that I must be awake.

What happened? I crack my eyes to find a searing blur of white and not much else and force myself to think, clenching my teeth against the pain. I remember losing the game. I remember the fight. The letter. Then things turn into a blur.

A groan rasps from my throat and I open my eyes the rest of the way. A hospital bed resolves into view. Two silhouettes flicker at the foot of the bed. I blink my eyes, focus, and swallow my shame with an aching throat. Eric and Dad are with me, hovering, eyes expectant and dark-ringed.

When they see I'm awake, Eric leans over me. My ribs

scream red and my skin is tender, but there's also relief. *Eric is here. Eric is here.*

"Eric?" I croak. I sound like a dead, broken thing.

"Yeah," he says. He squeezes my shoulder and Dad stands, his eyes wide with hope and fear, and together they fill up my whole dim vision. "We're here."

"Son," Dad says. "Oh my god, son, hey."

This is the second time I've seen him cry. He kisses my forehead. Runs his hands through my hair. If I could move much without wanting to puke or scream I might try to pull away, but as it is, I have to deal with it. I close my eyes and realize it actually feels kind of nice.

"I'm gonna go get coffee," Eric says. "Give you two time to talk."

I hear him leave the room and open my eyes again. Dad pulls a chair to the side of the bed and sits with a groan. I remember suddenly how I wished for him to go away and feel even sicker.

"Doctor says you're lucky," Dad says. He rubs his eyes and smiles at me, though the lines around his eyes and mouth betray a deep fatigue. "As far as he can tell, there's no long-term effects. They got you here just in time."

"Lucky you found me," I say. It doesn't *feel* lucky. Right now, in this moment, I don't want to die quite as much, but I still feel like it would have been better if I had.

"I didn't," Dad says. I blink in surprise. He shrugs. "I was on my way back from Nashville with the car…"

"Then how… ?"

"Eric found you," Dad says. I'll have to process that later, because right now all I can think of are the last things I said to him, and I can't deal with feeling like a monster on top of feeling like literal shit. "Thank god for him."

"Yeah."

"Now listen," Dad says. He wipes his eyes and does an admirable job collecting himself. "I'm taking all the blame on this one." I start to say something, but he glares at me, so I clamp my mouth shut. "I ignored warning signs. I've got my excuses, but I don't accept excuses from my students and I won't accept them from myself. I failed you, and I'm sorry, and it's time to make it right."

"Okay," I say. Where did *this* Dad come from? There's always been coach Dad and home Dad, and I've never seen them fused like this before.

"I will *not* lose you too." He shakes his head and clenches his fists. "I just won't. So you're gonna do exactly what I say, all right?"

"All right…"

"Therapy starts next week," he says. "Therapy for you, therapy for me, and therapy for both of us together. We're going full-court press on this."

I can't help smiling despite the circumstances. Of course he's approaching this like a coach.

"And no more football," he says. I roll my eyes even

though it hurts. He looks thoughtful. "Were you *trying* to get kicked off the team?"

"I don't know," I say. "Not on purpose. Maybe."

"You don't want to play football," he says.

I turn from him and stare out into the hall. The urge to lie is still there, but as I squeeze a fistful of blanket in my good hand I realize it's beyond pointless now.

"No," I say.

"Why'd you start again then?" he says. I shrug, mostly because in retrospect my reasoning seems pretty insane. "Okay. Well, why didn't you tell me you wanted to quit?"

"It made you happy," I say.

"For Christ's sake, son," he says, "you being *alive* makes me happy. You're my kid."

"Okay," I say. I suddenly feel infinitely small and stupid. He rubs his temple and sighs.

The hospital machines beep around us, filling the silence. I hear a nurse pushing a cart down the hallway. I turn towards Dad as much as I can, my cheek scraping against the rough cotton pillow. He looks straight into my eyes.

"I know there's more to what happened tonight than just football. You can tell me that when you're ready. But for now, let's just get you home."

My pulse hammers in my chest, afraid that he'll keep pushing me. Or hopeful that he will. Isn't that what I've been desperate for this whole time?

"I'll tell you soon," I say.

Dad scratches his chin and looks up at the ceiling, a thoughtful little rumble emanating from his chest. "Okay, son. That's all I can ask."

I breathe out a sigh of relief. I'm not ready yet. I need the words, and I need to figure out what stops me from saying them, but I have to get there. What other choice is there?

He stands and says, "I'll go get Eric now."

My head falls back onto the pillow and there's a period of drowsy meditation, maybe thirty seconds, maybe an hour. I don't know. Eric's distant voice pulls me back up and I see that his shirt is a wrinkled, stained mess, his eyes haunted in a way that punches through everything to fill me with sadness. How could my Eric look that way? He's always been so carefree, so lackadaisical, even in a place that should have ground those qualities out of him. *Who* would be monstrous enough to shake him like this?

But then I start to remember.

"You're back," I say, my voice raspy.

"How'd your talk go?" Eric says as he stares down at me. I look up into his face, half exhausted and half desperate cheer, and I can see he's been crying. I look at my bandaged knuckles and shame adds to the crust of pain and filth clogging every part of me.

"Good," I say. I start to ask how he found me, but what explanation could there be? He's my Eric, and I needed him, and he was there.

"That's good," he says. He picks at the bed of his thumbnail, coughs, and finds something interesting in the corner to look at.

"I'm sorry."

"I'm sorry too," Eric says.

I take as deep a breath as I can. Maybe now's the time to tell him. But as I try to find the courage to tell Eric, I finally understand that maybe courage was never the problem. Maybe the problem is that *I* hate this thing about myself, so I assume everyone else will too. But Eric? The Eric who sits through hours of movies he doesn't like? The Eric who came over to hang out, even when all I did was lie in a field and be quiet next to him? The Eric who knew to find me? The Eric here, next to me, now?

There's more to it, and less, and all of it through a medicated haze, but in this quiet moment I resolve that I *will* tell him who I really am, who I want to become. I'll tell *everyone*.

"There's something I've never told you."

"I know," he says. "I should have pushed harder or looked closer or—"

"There was nothing you could have done or said," I say. I squeeze his hand as hard as I can, which isn't very hard. "Eric, I put myself through hell to avoid it. *You* couldn't have made me tell you. But I will. Soon. I promise."

"Okay," he says. He squeezes me back and smiles weakly. "If you say so," Eric says. His eyes slide shut and he leans forward, pressing my fingers to his forehead. "I was so afraid. *So* afraid. What would I do without you?"

"Cultivate a hobby?" I say. The sniffling gets louder and I realize his shoulders are shaking. "No. Hey. Don't…"

He looks up, his tear-streaked face startlingly resolute. Part of me thinks I should pull my hand back at some point, but the rest of me thinks it's fine to let him decide how long he wants to hold it. Our eyes linger. I realize his thumb is tracing the lines in my palm and decide not to say anything. Eventually his eyes dart to the door, ensuring it's closed maybe, and then back to mine. "Listen."

"Hmm?"

"I …"

Say it, I think. *Please say it.*

"You're not allowed to die," he says. "Okay?"

I squeeze his hand one last time before slipping mine free and resting it in my lap.

"Okay," I promise him. "Okay."

SEVENTEENTH
BIRTHDAY

ERIC

My fingers hurt as I push down on the guitar strings, but it's a good kind of pain. That's maybe the only helpful thing football has taught me, that some kinds of pain equal progress.

Of course, I *should* be at football practice, but fat chance there. Maybe my best friend almost dying and my family disintegrating forced me to reassess my priorities. It's still early enough in the school year that homework's light, and I figured I deserved an afternoon to myself. The sun pours into my window, and it's a perfect September day, not as hot as it could be but still bright and worthy of short sleeves. The house is quiet, and I have it all to myself.

The last year has been strange. No Peyton, barely a word from Isaac, and my parents constantly at each other's throats. Then, finally, Mom moved out a month ago. As she left, Mom pulled me into a hug that made me realize how small she was. My chest muffled her voice, but she said we could talk about me coming to stay with her after the holidays, that for now the fall semester was too close and she didn't want to interfere with school. I didn't realize she'd been crying until she was gone and I saw the dark spots on my shirt.

Then I found the divorce paperwork in Dad's office downstairs.

Hard to pin down exactly why *that* made football seem irrelevant, but it did.

I kick my feet up on the bed and pull my guitar further up onto my lap. I lay two fingers across the second fret for picking practice, twanging every other string down then up, over and over, faster and faster until I mess up. Then I start over. Of course, I want to quit and watch YouTube or text Morgan or listen to my new playlist, but even more than that, I want to be good at playing guitar, and the gap between talent and skill is discipline.

I haven't spoken to Morgan in a few days, and after everything that happened last year, that's become more okay – normal. I know Morgan needs his space, and he knows I'm there for him. Before, when we would go long stretches without talking, that weird pressure would build up at the back of my neck. But I don't get that weird ache any more. We're already seventeen. Already seniors. And we've only got so much time left before high school ends. I think about all the movie nights, concerts, and nights stargazing we'll *never* get back. Football practice, and all the time it's eaten up in my life, just feels petty in comparison.

More and more I've been doing what I *want* to do instead of what I *should* do. I skip lunch, bike instead of drive, and use all the money I save on gas for guitar lessons. The calorie deficit's cost me muscle and being seen on a bike instead of in my car has lost me clout, but my new music instructor, a retired session guitarist from Nashville who teaches out of a strip mall, says I'm good and getting better.

I haven't told Morgan I'm playing again, though. I'm worried it'll remind him of his mom, since she's the one who first bought me a guitar and sheet music. He's been in such a better place this year that I don't want to pull him back into that darkness.

My phone buzzes. I rest my guitar on my shoulder, check it, and see Susan's name on the screen. I feel like an asshole for not wanting to respond. She hasn't done anything wrong, and I don't think I've done anything wrong, but month by month things feel more out of tune between us.

Happy birthday, Susan's text reads. *Excited for tonight?*

Yeah, I type. *Hey, I'm busy at practice, can I talk to you later?*

There's a pause before she types back, *k*, which feels a little weird, but I push off the thought as I hear the garage door open and heavy footsteps downstairs. It can only be one person. I turn back to the window and keep playing.

My bedroom door opens and Dad walks in. I refuse to turn around.

I'd hoped he would chill now that Mom's gone, but now I see Mom was a lightning rod. She protected us as much as she could.

Not for the first time I imagine Peyton in his new life in Miami, sharing a loft with his girlfriend above the restaurant where he works, most of his rough edges sanded off after two years of freedom, and feel a little jealous.

"Why aren't you at practice?" Dad's voice shoots through me like an arrow, his tone low and dangerous.

I spin my chair around and there he is, home early from the car lot, red-eyed and sallow.

"It got cancelled," I lie, trying for nonchalance. I've never been a good liar.

"Drove by the field on the way home," Dad says. "It sure didn't *look* cancelled."

"I mean," I say. I try to look pathetic and fake a cough. "I had to cancel. Is what I mean. I'm feeling sick."

"It's your birthday," he says, his voice cold and flat, "so I'm gonna pretend you didn't just lie and then keep lying after I caught you." He reaches me in two steps and takes my guitar, and I don't try to stop him. At least he's not yelling.

"Hey!" I start to stand, but he looms over me, eyes

narrowing, and I sit back down.

"Watch your tone," he says. He tosses the guitar on my bed and I wince at his rough handling.

"Yes, sir…"

"I can't hear you," Dad says.

"Yes, sir!" I say. It's not worth fighting with him when he's like this.

"Went too easy on you," he says. "That's the problem. You were the youngest, so I let your mother baby you. But she's not here."

Because of you, I think. He watches me for a moment and I feel like a bug under a pair of tweezers.

"Anyway," he says. "You got birthday plans tonight, or are you waiting for the weekend?"

"Probably just gonna hang out with Morgan," I say, knowing I should have tried to lie again.

His eyes narrow as he moves back to the doorway and shoves his hands in his pockets. I can see what Dad's thinking.

Over the last year, I've noticed something, and of course Dad has seen it too: the way Morgan unconsciously crosses his legs at the thigh and flips his hair when he laughs, the way his voice lilts and flows more and more when he talks, the way his hands dance as he makes a point…he's different now. More…alive. He still really loves horror movies and metal, though. That'll always be quintessential Morgan.

"You should really think about what kinds of people you surround yourself with," Dad says.

"He's my best friend," I say. I have to force myself not to scowl or let anger seep into my voice.

"I know that seems important now," he says, "but you've got your whole life ahead of you. If you let Morgan get between you and the team, you could lose a shot at recruitment. And people could get ideas. Your girlfriend could get ideas."

"My girlfriend knows I'm not gay," I say, and now I can't help rolling my eyes.

"Watch your tone," Dad says.

"Yes, sir…"

"If I start to see you slacking on the field because of that boy, I'm going to put my foot down," Dad says, pointing a finger at me. "I can't stop you from seeing him at school, but I sure as hell can make sure you never see him outside."

"Yes, sir," I reply again, my voice automatic – trained. My face is a mask but my insides feel like they're on fire. I hate that he thinks he can talk to me that way. And I hate that there's nothing I can do about it. But I haven't survived in this house for this long by letting him get to me.

He nods, apparently satisfied, and turns to leave. I reach to pick up my guitar from the bed and accidentally ping a string. The sound vibrates through the room.

Dad pauses in the doorway, his wide back rising and falling.

"I don't have a lot of warnings left in me," he says, not even looking at me. "Get your shit together."

MORGAN

My therapist Judith's office is nestled in a strip mall between a pet groomer and a nail salon. I park my car, the one Mom gave me last year on my birthday. It's a beater but I love it more than anything I've ever owned. Having a car has meant having freedom, and that's what I've needed the most this past year. I glance at the console clock and notice that I'm early for my appointment. My three-year-old iPod's playing "Rome" and I decide to let Yeasayer finish before I head inside. The car hums beneath me, the old leather seats hugging my body.

I still haven't been able to tell anyone but Judith and her assistant, Gavin, that I'm trans, though the people in my support group have assumed and I haven't corrected them. I couldn't even tell the psychiatrist at the mental hospital, but I feel pretty blameless in that – I didn't really want to talk to anyone but Dad and Eric after what happened, and a hospital wing full of strangers and a hulking room-mate who wouldn't stop talking about fire wasn't exactly a healing environment.

Mom's car has allowed me to drive into Nashville for support groups where I've gotten to meet other trans people, some of them still in the closet like me, some of them my age and already transitioning, and a couple in their twenties with, like, actual lives and boyfriends and girlfriends.

To be honest, it was kind of hard to be around them, at first. To watch them ignore the ways their bodies and voices betrayed them. But every month I see a little bit more of the beauty in these people like me. It feels like I'm on the cusp of something, a chrysalis just on the verge of cracking.

It isn't always easy. I still have bad days, when my skull feels like it's full of bees and my heart is empty and all I want to do is lie on my back and melt into the pavement for ever, only now Dad can tell when it's happening and I'll watch a brittle panic wash over him. It makes me feel guilty for being depressed, and I get frustrated sometimes, but I do my best not to fight with him. I even think he might be dating again – if his occasional late nights and the receipts for movies and restaurants I find when I do laundry are any indication. I'm not sure how I feel about that. I tell myself that I'm happy if he's happy.

Watching Eric's family disintegrate has reminded me

how lucky I am, at least in this one way – what would my life be like if Carson were my dad? Jasmine's parents got divorced a few years ago, and she's been walking me through what Eric needs and doesn't need while he goes through this: let him talk about it at his own pace and just hang out with him so he knows I'm there for him. The last one's been hard because of his football practice and my film club and yearbook committee, but I'm trying my best.

I try not to think of how little time we have left together before life pulls us in different directions. Used to be, I assumed Eric would head off to play college football like Isaac did before he was drafted by the Seahawks, and I would stay here to rot in Thebes. Maybe I'd get to see Eric when he came home for Christmas and try to hide how much I resented his life while I plugged away behind a gas station counter or whatever. *Now* I'm the one thinking about film school. I'm the one who looks like they're going to get out of this place. That maybe Eric will stay behind.

Either way, we'll have a distance between us that's never existed before.

The song finishes and I switch off my iPod and turn off the car.

Taking a breath, I force a smile and wave to my therapist's assistant as I slam my car door closed. Gavin is a broad-shouldered, bearded graduate student from University of Tennessee, Knoxville who's doing some kind of survey of LGBT mental health in the South.

"Hey, girl," he says, as a grin cracks his face.

At the word *girl* I feel a flush of warmth in my neck and back.

"Hey, Gavin," I say as I pop the door open with my hip.

"Cool haircut," he says as he follows me inside.

I reach up to touch my hair, a messy bob with dark brown highlights, for maybe the three hundredth time in the last twenty-four hours. It felt risky asking Jasmine to give me a girlish haircut, but unless I style it, I think it looks a bit like Kurt Cobain's hair. When I did style it, in the bathroom alone, it looked more like a sort of Joan Jett kind of thing. My heart ached as I watched my reflection in the mirror, the wispy brown strands framing my face, the idea that I could be a woman like she's a woman.

"Thanks," I say. "My friend Jasmine did it." I think, not for the first time since it happened, about how readily she took me back, and how supportive she's been.

"The doc's last appointment cancelled," Gavin says, pulling me out of my thoughts.

We head down the hallway and then through the door that leads to Judith's lobby. "Hello, Morgan," Judith says when we reach the door. Her voice sounds like a school librarian mixed with iron, but I learned not to be intimidated months ago.

She's reading someone's file over the tops of her thick-rimmed black glasses. Dirty-blond hair falls over her shoulders and down her back in oscillating waves, shot through with bright silver. I knew I would like her the first time I saw her lobby. Judith's office walls were decorated with B-movie posters, everything from *Forbidden Planet* to *The Blob* to *Plan 9 From Outer Space*. There's even a signed photo of Vincent Price in the bathroom, his piercing gaze following my every move. I had expected, I don't know, motivational posters, daily affirmations, maybe some prayer guides and Bibles.

Thebes isn't the middle of nowhere but it isn't *somewhere*, you know?

I once asked Judith if it was okay to have those posters up, if people found them weird. She laughed and said, "Nobody identifies more with monsters than LGBT people and the mentally ill. My clients tend to be both. I think it helps reassure them there's no normalcy here to worry about violating." And then she winked. "Plus, what's the point of owning a business if you can't decorate it how you want. Right?"

And after months of coming here, of feeling safe in this space, I agree with her.

Judith checks her watch as I approach. "Let's head back to the lab."

"The lab" is an office arrayed with scented candles, stim toys like kinetic sand and bubble wrap, and an array of overstuffed, earth-tone furniture. Relaxing music burbles from a speaker somewhere nearby while incense burns on the table between us. She hands me a mug of coffee, my favourite drink since getting sober, and falls into a papasan with a cup of tea clasped in both hands.

"Happy birthday, Morgan," she says as she settles in and pulls out her notebook.

"Thanks," I say. Unlike past years, I've been counting down to this day. Seventeen marks the year when I want to make a change – to finally tell the world who I truly am – inside and out. I still don't know what my future will look like, but this birthday I want to take a step in the right direction. Judith watches me as I sink into the big, cosy chair across from her. Her eyes are dark and deep as the ocean at night, something a person could fall into if they aren't careful. It was hard not to be unnerved by her at first, but she was the only therapist I could find within reasonable driving distance who handled "gender and sexuality" so I gave it a shot.

"So," Judith says as we begin our session. "I have a birthday surprise for you."

I make a curious sound and she smiles, which is rare for her.

"You asked last month about referrals for hormones. Is that still something you're interested in?"

I nod slowly and chew the inside of my cheek. I'd be lying if I said I wasn't nervous – surgeries and medications are scary even when they're something you need. "Yes," I hear my voice say, almost detached from my body. I can't believe I just said yes, but the answer is yes.

237

"Well then," she says. "Let's do this."

"Really?" I ask, breathless.

"I've got no professional reservations, and your referral is ready to go. There's a doctor I know in Nashville covered by your father's insurance."

She hands me a letter that's been tucked into her notebook. My lips part but no sound comes out. Her smile shifts to a look of concern and then horror as she reaches out. I realize I'm about to drop my mug and catch it at the last minute. I laugh. I can't stop laughing.

What does it feel like for something good to happen in your life? Ask me that five minutes ago and I'd have shrugged. Now I know: it's a weightlessness, a shaking, electric tingle across my whole body. My body – not a machine, not a thing I inhabit, but the cells and muscles and bone of which I am made and which are me.

"I'll just need your dad to sign off," Judith says, watching me carefully. "Since you're under eighteen."

And there's the catch. I close my eyes and click my teeth, biting back the swears trying to climb from me.

"What's the matter?" she says.

"I'll have to tell him," I say.

"That's the idea," Judith says. "But I thought you said he was supportive?"

"About not wanting me to die, yeah. Nothing about gender," I say. I lean forward. "I mean, where would he have even heard about trans people? Mean jokes on TV?"

238

I rub my eyes and take a sharp breath. "Listen," I say. "I used to have five people in my life who knew me from the *moment* I was born. Now I have two. I'm not sure I can handle losing another one. And…"

"And what?" Judith says. She must notice the way my eyes are twitching because she nudges a box of Kleenex in my direction, but I've got it under control.

"Nothing," I say instead. "I'm being stupid."

"You're not being stupid," Judith says with a frown. "Even if a concern isn't logical, the feeling is valid. Don't be so hard on yourself."

Judith is right, and this is something I've wanted to do for a long time. "With the hormones… If I go through with this…what about…" I pause. "The future? I've never felt like I had one before…" I sigh and run my finger up the side of the mug. "What happens as I get older? Like, I can imagine existing as an adult, sort of, if this whole thing works out. But now that I want to live – I *want* to *live*. How's a career going to work? How's love going to work? God, how's *sex* going to work?"

Judith looks at me, taking everything I say seriously. "I'd be lying if I said your gender won't affect these things, but you have to make the right choice for you. Even though it feels like everything is going to be so hard, in lots of ways it'll feel better to live honestly. The important thing is to be able to trust your support system. You need people who accept you and love you." She gives me a reassuring smile. "Your father and Eric are a good start. The rest will come."

"Yeah," I say. "*Yeah...*"

"Good luck, Morgan," she says. "You'll do fine tonight."

As I leave the office, Gavin wishes me happy birthday. All I can manage in return is a nod as I pass under the portraits of monsters. Standing in the parking lot, I look at nothing and everything all at once. There's a wind from the north, crisp with the warning of an early chill as it drags at the weakening trees, and under their rustle I can just make out the distant hum of the interstate, where thousands of unknown hearts hurtle every day to and from places I'd kill to go.

I've never thought much about the supernatural except when I'm at my worst – Mom didn't make us go to church – but it occurs to me this place might be dying from more than just drugs and closed mines. Maybe a town has a soul. Maybe all the ways people like me have suffered turned Thebes sour a long time ago. I used to think the interstate was the finishing blow, but what if it's the universe unfurling a rope ladder for people who need to get out?

I start Mom's car, hook my iPod back into the aux cord, and blast "Bulletproof Heart" as I pull out of the parking lot and head home. I need to tell Eric, and I need to tell him tonight.

ERIC

No way in hell am I staying at the house after that "conversation" with Dad. There's no dealing with him when he's like this. The door chimes as I step into Taco Bell. It's probably the only new building that Thebes has seen in ten years. There used to be another Taco Bell across town, but then a tornado came through last November, touching down at random, like God tapping an impatient finger. Nobody I knew was hurt, thankfully, but houses were swept away, along with the old Taco Bell and the Blockbuster where Morgan and I would wander for hours. Now there's nowhere to go to rent movies except the library, and that's not exactly the best hangout spot.

This new Taco Bell is all black and chrome, all open space rather than the frosted glass partitions I remember from the old one. Everything's changing, me along with it. I take my place in line and watch a kid I recognize from school pressing quesadillas.

I've stood still for so long – my whole life. My feet planted right where Dad wanted them to be, all in the hope that if I did everything right then everything would turn out all right. To me, the universe was a simple machine where a person put in effort and compliance and got out peace and happiness. But then there was Morgan's suicide attempt, and then the divorce, and now I understand that effort and outcome have nothing much to do with each other.

Morgan's mom, Donna, was one of the nicest people I ever knew. Now she's dead. Morgan worked harder than I ever did at football, and I think he really used to love it, but forcing himself into that role almost killed him. I think Mom might have spent my whole life trying to hold our family together against the tectonic force of Dad's ego, and now she's god knows where. It's all chaos, and the rain soaks everybody, and if you think about it too hard, it's almost too cruel to bear.

But what were the odds two families as different as mine and Morgan's would have weaved together the way they did, if only for the time they did? What were the odds of that snowstorm seventeen years ago? Of two families trapped in the hospital? Maybe that's what life is about: surviving what you can't control and clinging to the good things the winds whip up.

Grabbing my tacos, I find a sunlit corner booth and I open my laptop when a text from Morgan comes in.

Hey, it reads. *Happy birthday! I know we didn't make solid plans, but what's your current sitch? No rush, but obviously I have to see you before midnight. There's something I want to tell you. In person.*

Something he wants to tell me? I immediately worry that something's wrong, but it doesn't feel like that's the case, and I've learned to trust my gut where he's concerned. I eat a taco and stare out the glass window. A crow hops on the pavement, chasing away sparrows in its search for food. I swallow even though I don't feel hungry any more.

I want to be a good friend. I want to be trusted, and to know what's wrong. I start to text Morgan back when the restaurant door opens and familiar voices bubble through it.

"And she still has a flip phone," Tina, one of the cheerleaders, says with a cruel laugh as she walks towards the register. "Can you imagine? Come *on*."

The other girls laugh. I look up with a wince to find Susan and her friends. She notices me and confusion passes over her face, then anger. I wave and force a smile. She crosses the dining room through shafts of golden afternoon light, every inch the beauty who swept me off my feet two years ago. Without even a hello, she sits across from me, adjusting her ponytail.

243

"What the hell, Eric?" she says, her voice low. "What are you even doing here?"

I look down at my hands and pick the callus on one of my fingertips, caught in my own lie. "Practice ended early?"

"Seriously?" she says. She folds her hands and looks down at them, then back up at me with a hard stare. "Could you at least do me the favour of lying well? I know you weren't at practice. We dropped by the field so Adria could grab something from Nate. I'd hoped that you'd at least have the decency to give me a good excuse." She rubs the bridge of her nose and shakes her head. "You could have just said, 'It's my birthday and I didn't want to go.'"

"Well," I say meekly. I brush a few crumbs off the table as my gaze drifts out to the parking lot and the street beyond. "It is my birthday, and I didn't want to go…"

"And if you hadn't lied that would be fine. More or less," Susan says. She smiles but it doesn't reach her eyes. "What's up with you, Eric?"

I sigh.

"I don't want to play football any more," I say, almost embarrassed to admit it, especially to her, because we both know what it means – no football equals no scholarships, and no scholarship means we're not going to college together. Her lips twist in understanding.

"Okay." There's a moment where her voice tightens and cracks, and she rubs her eyes once. Her lips thin into a line. I'm afraid she might cry. But then she breathes in sharply and nods slowly. "I get it."

"You do?" I ask sheepishly.

"This isn't working," she says. Her voice sounds dull. She buries the lower half of her face in folded arms and looks down at the table.

"What's not working?" I say nervously.

"Us. Together." She winces.

"Wait. Are you breaking up with me?" I say.

"I guess maybe I am," Susan replies.

My fingers comb through my hair and I let out a long, sputtering, tired breath. I think of Mom and Dad suddenly, and all their screaming matches over the years. My head fills with images of Mom packing a suitcase, tears streaming down her face while Dad stomps after her. There were the knock-down-drag-out fights and silences that I could only escape from with music. Something in me keeps waiting for one of us to scream and I feel like I *should* at least be mad at her for doing this on my birthday of all days, but I can't build up the anger. I don't want to make her stay in something she doesn't want to be in, and if I'm being honest, I don't think I want to be in this either.

We sit in silence for a long time. I notice her friends have settled across the room and they're not even trying to hide their stares. My face starts to burn as I imagine what they must think of me.

Susan rubs her neck, smiles softly, and shrugs. "What

do you say we end on a high note?" she says. I give her a confused look as she stands and smoothes her skirt. Then she's around the table, leaning down, brushing her bangs to the side, and with a soft little noise, she kisses my temple. "You were always very kind, Eric. For what it's worth." I feel my face turning pink. "I won't regret that it was you."

"D-ditto," I say, my voice cracking a little. "All of that, ditto. And you've been more patient with me than I think I deserve."

"Maybe," Susan says with a tired sigh, and then she's backing away. "Anyway. Are you quitting outright, or will I see you at the game next week?"

"I don't know," I say.

"Well then. See you around, I guess…"

"Yeah," I say.

She walks back to her friends and they huddle, speaking rapidly in urgent whispers. I throw away my trash, make my way to the exit, and as I near the door, Susan gives me one last look goodbye.

MORGAN

I get home from therapy to find that Dad has left Mom's present on the counter. It's a small box wrapped in wax paper and bound with butcher's twine. I pick it up, noticing it's heavier than I expected, and take a deep breath. Last year, her letter about the car nearly unravelled me – did unravel me – and part of me is afraid of what this year will bring. I remind myself I'm stronger today than I was a year ago. I can handle it.

I take the present to the front steps and open it with care, peeling back the wrapping paper. A small leather journal rests in my hands, older than I am, with its corners faded and curling and its pages yellowed. The nameplate on the front reads, *Top Secret Donna ~~Steiner~~ Gardner Culinary Technology. Do Not Steal.* I open it with trembling fingers and find the names of dishes I haven't had in for ever: fried green tomatoes, buttermilk biscuits, devilled eggs, squash and bacon casserole. Years of microwaved food and takeout leave my mouth watering at memories of family meals, steaming and fragrant around the table in our old kitchen. Grief starts to rot the memories, but then I flip to a middle page and a note falls out.

Morgan,
Here's hoping you inherited my talent in the kitchen and not your father's. If the worst comes to pass and you can't boil water without starting a fire, well, you can give this to your wife someday. Still, wherever I am when you read this, it would make me happy for you to at least try making a few things before giving up. Wish I could write more but I've been tiring out so easily lately. I know you know I love you, but I still want to remind you. I love you. I'll always love you.

And speaking of love, take a look at this recipe. I'm not saying it makes people fall in love with you, but I did make some for your father when we'd just started dating. Maybe it was my natural beauty and charm that seduced him, but I'm pretty sure it was the cake.

Love,
Mom

I investigate the marked page and find the entry for German chocolate cake. The margins are filled with hearts and Mom's handwriting warns caution across the top and bottom. I wipe my eyes and laugh, but then an idea flashes. No matter what happens tonight, Eric and I need a birthday cake.

Turns out, baking is actually easy. It's like chemistry class or cleaning a camera. All I have to do is make sure I have the exact measurements and follow the directions. My phone buzzes as I slide the dark chocolate cake onto our rickety oven rack. I wash flour from my hands and look at the screen. It's Eric.

Hey. Sorry for the delay. Happy birthday. We can talk whenever.

Hey you! Cool cool cool. Movie marathon at your place?

Carson might be miserable to be around lately, but his house dependably has working air-conditioning and it's usually clean. Which is better than Dad and I can say for our trailer.

There's a pause and then he writes: *Sure. Cool.*

This is fine. This is *fine*.

Great, I type. *See you in an hour?* I stare at the draft for a moment and then add, *And hey. Are you okay?*

It's fine, he types. *I'll see you in an hour!*

He said, "It's fine," not, "I'm fine." The words set me off, but I know I can ask him in person soon enough.

Thirty minutes later, the timer dings and I take the cake out of the oven to cool. The smell of chocolate and coconut wafts through the trailer, making everything feel warm and cosy against the chill September afternoon.

I manage not to burn my hands on the cake tin – not even a little bit – and I tell myself to take that as a sign that tonight is going to be okay.

ERIC

I drop my phone on the passenger seat and lean my chin to the steering wheel, the Walmart parking lot monopolizing my vision like a hypnotic black wasteland from some dystopian movie.

My fingers absent-mindedly scan through the radio, through random, fuzzy channels. If I'm being honest, Susan dumping me isn't the darkest cloud in my life, but I feel slightly guilty thinking that. At least I'll see Morgan in an hour. That's something. Silver linings, right?

My phone lights up and starts to buzz a few minutes later, and tension rolls through me because who even *calls* anyone any more? But then I see Peyton's name.

"Hey, hey, hey," I say as I pick up and turn the music down. I try to sound cheerful.

"Hey, man," Peyton says. He sounds nervous, which is weird for him. "Happy birthday."

"Thanks," I say. "What'd you get me?"

"Cheque's in the mail," he says. "How are you?"

"My girlfriend dumped me," I reply, aiming for nonchalance.

"Aw hell," Peyton says. I hear a grunt and then the rattle of a fire escape, followed by the click and hiss of a cigarette being lit. "I was just gonna talk for a minute, but lay it on me."

"It's not a big deal," I say.

"Sure it isn't," Peyton says. "Sure, sure. What'd you do?"

"Nothing," I say.

"Yeah, dude," Peyton says. "Sometimes I'll do 'nothing' and me and Chelsea'll fight about it for days."

"No," I say. "Literally, I was doing *nothing* and she didn't like it. Or I was doing the wrong nothings."

"I get it. Sucks either way even if it's for the best. But, uh, hey! There was something I wanted to tell you."

"Shoot."

"It's…it's hard to say this, and I know you're gonna be cool, but…" I focus on his voice. "I've …uh, I've seen a lot the last two years, man. Met a bunch of people. Done some thinking. And I'm ashamed I put this off, but I owe you an apology."

"An apology?" I don't know how else to reply, but all the same I feel light on my feet. Isaac's been a nonentity since he moved to Seattle, and the one time I was able to get him on the phone after Mom left, I sort of got the impression he was siding with Dad. The idea that he lived in the same house with the same parents and came to *that* conclusion made me too angry to see straight, but instead of cussing him out, I dropped the call and haven't spoken to him since.

"There are reasons I acted like I acted. You know some of 'em, but I won't go into the others because those aren't your problem."

"Well," I say. "Thanks, man. That...actually means a lot to hear."

"Good," he says. "So, any plans tonight?"

"Hanging out with Morgan," I say, feeling slightly nervous as the name leaves my mouth.

"God," Peyton says. "That kid. If I ever see him again I gotta apologize to him too."

I smile sadly. That's true. It'll probably never happen, but this is a good start. It's nice feeling like I have at least one brother in my corner, but if you'd told me four years ago that it would end up being Peyton I would have assumed you were insane.

"Yeah." The line goes quiet again. "Anyway, dude, I won't keep you. Before I go though, one more thing, and this is so corny and so, gah...lame, but bear with me."

"Okay, man." I chuckle.

"I think, of the three of us, you're probably the best man," he says. "Boy. Young man. Whatever. Like, the

253

most decent. I wanna say the softest, but in a good way. And I worry a lot about you being alone with Dad."

"I'll be fine," I say. I start to add, "What's the worst he could do?" but stop. Peyton knows the worst he can do better than any of us.

"Yeah well," Peyton says, suddenly serious. "You've got my number. I'm gonna send you Chelsea's number in case I'm ever not available. If anything ever does happen, you call me."

"Peyton…"

"I need an affirmative on this one."

"Okay," I say. "Yeah. Sure. I'll call."

"Good," he says. "Love you. Happy birthday."

"Love…you too?" I say, but he's already hung up. I try to remember the last time he said that to me but, as I start the engine, nothing comes to mind.

MORGAN

I *could* just not tell Eric. What's a promise if I only made it to myself and my therapist? Easily broken is what it is. I'm standing on Eric's front porch with a cake in my arms thinking about death, hoping his neighbours can't see the way my knees shake. My mouth feels dry. I raise my hand to knock, but before I can the door opens, and there he is in a Joy Division T-shirt and tight jeans, his curls glittering in the afternoon light.

"Oh!" Eric says. There's a moment of blinking surprise and then he smiles wide. What if this is the last time I see that smile? "There you are. I had a feeling." His eyes drift down to the cake and go wide. "Whoa."

"Surprise," I say, wobbling it theatrically while being careful not to drop it.

He leads me inside and I slide the cake onto the counter while he rummages in the silverware drawer and produces a knife. I catch a glimpse of his dad futzing with the mower through the back patio door.

"Surprised he's not making you mow the lawn," I say. *Why am I bringing up Carson?* Since my suicide attempt he's said maybe two words to me that weren't grunts.

"We had a fight," Eric says. "Sort of."

"Do you wanna talk about it? Is that why things were just 'fine' earlier?"

"Nah," he says. It comes out clipped and flat, and I flinch because the tone's so unlike him. The pressure thumps at my neck again, and for a moment my own anxiety is overwhelmed with the need to hug him. But I stop myself, worried how Eric will feel about my touch when he finds out what I'm about to tell him.

I look around the kitchen and realize that most of Jenny's things are gone – her wedding china and the cookbooks that used to line the counter. Maybe she sent for them when she got where she was going, or maybe Carson put them in storage. Maybe he destroyed what he could and dumped the rest. That certainly sounds like him. The house is still clean without her, but sad without all Jenny's little touches. Our trailer might be messy, and the dishes might sit in the sink for days sometimes, but at least there's life there.

Eric pauses before he cuts into the cake and looks at me with sudden awe.

"Hold on," he says. "Did you *make* this?"

I shove my hands in my hoodie pockets, look down at my shoes, and nod. It suddenly seems stupid to have baked and brought a cake. Like, what, I'm going to tell him I'm a girl, but look, cake. Stupid. Pathetic. Not for the first time I wonder if I want to be a girl because I'm a failure at everything. Perhaps I just want to create a new self entirely and leave the mess of this life behind. My eyes squeeze shut. That explanation has always been too easy – all the cruel explanations have always been too easy – and I know it.

Eric plants his hands on the counter and appraises the cake. The coconut didn't brown enough and the frosting isn't consistent, but it looks like a cake and smells like a cake and that's what counts. I guess. As I watch Eric inspect my creation a sunbeam of pride breaks through the clouds, but only for a moment before my nerves get me again.

"Can we eat upstairs?" I ask. "So we can talk? I'd rather avoid your dad, if that's okay."

"Sure. Right." Eric gives me a curious look, like he wants to know *what* I want to talk about, but I just give him a shrug. My heart beats in my ears.

He cuts us generous pieces and he inhales half his piece in the time it takes to mount the stairs. As we make our way to his room the weight of time pushes down on me. I feel surrounded by ghosts and memories. There's me and Eric in a laundry hamper, screaming as we slide down the stairs. There we are at the bottom, near the door, lacing our boots with preschooler hands in breathless anticipation of one of the two snow days we got that winter. There we are at the top, strangely proportioned, like all sixth graders, sprawled on the stairs, listening to music even though we got yelled at for being underfoot and there were a million better places to be.

I close my eyes as we sit, and I try to will the ghosts away. When I open my eyes, I find Eric looking directly at me, a worried expression on his face. I place my untouched cake on the desk and cross my legs.

Tell him.

I swallow so loud I feel like it echoes.

He plops onto the foot of the bed, chocolate smudged at the edges of his mouth as he unselfconsciously licks crumbs from his plate. I laugh despite everything.

"What?" he says.

"You've got…" I start to reach out to rub the chocolate away, but stop myself. I lean back against his pillows, my heart hammering, and gesture towards my own mouth.

He smirks and wipes his face with the back of his arm.

"Okay," he says. He sets his plate on the comforter next to him and his face grows serious. "What's up, Morgan?"

"Before I say what…" My voice shakes so bad. "I just. Wanted to check. Are you doing okay? You can tell me if the fight with your dad was bad or if you're just feeling upset or…"

"Susan broke up with me," he says. His face betrays a little sadness, but then he shrugs.

"Seriously?" I ask, although the news isn't that surprising. If I were his girlfriend, and he blew me off as much as he's blown her off, I'd probably break up with him too. "What happened?"

"The specifics?" he says. "I lied to her about skipping practice. I haven't been prioritizing her. The flame's just kinda gone. But…I don't know, I guess she had a plan for the sort of person both of us were gonna become, together, and I veered off course." Sadness creeps into his voice and I do my best to listen. "I didn't mean for that to happen, though. It just happened." He sighs and crosses his legs. "I don't think we have much choice in who we turn out to be, as much as we might want to."

"Yes," I say, surprised by my own intensity. "Yes. I think that too." I swallow.

The thing is, after all this time I still don't really know how to put this into words. I've tried so many ways, rehearsed this conversation so *many* times. Do I say I was born in the wrong body? A girl trapped in a boy's body? Do I even *believe* in souls, or girl brains and boy brains? But if I say, "I *am* a girl," doesn't that kind of fly in the face of my present circumstances, how people see me *now*? How everyone has always seen me? On the other hand, doesn't "I want to be a girl" almost make it sound like play-acting? I realize I'm chewing my thumbnail.

"Morgan?"

"I'm transgender," I say. It just comes out. My mouth snaps shut and my eyes go wide as I watch his eyebrows curl together and his mouth pucker up.

Oh god.

It's happening.

A jolt of pain shoots up my arm and I realize I've drawn blood biting my thumb. The distant sound of the mower stops, and a corner of his Coheed and Cambria poster flaps in the wind from his fan.

Eric doesn't say anything. He just sits there staring at me, looking mad, or thoughtful, or I don't know, because my brain won't slow down for even a second. I scrape my nails along my jeans and clear my throat, unable to stand one more second of the quiet. "Do you know what that means?"

"I. Um. I think so?" he says. His words come out on a drip feed. "You mean you were born a girl but you've been living as a boy this whole—"

"No!" I rub my cheek and look around the room, vulnerability crawling across my skin. It's like one of those dreams where I realize I'm naked at school, only it's worse than that, much worse.

"Okay," he says. He forces a smile. It must be forced. "I was gonna say, we used to take baths together and the memories are fuzzy but I would have noticed—"

"*Anyway,*" I say. I look down at my knees and let out

another breath. That's…an amusing mistake for him to have made. It's a little funny. Or stupid. Either way it's enough to pull me back from the brink a few steps. "It's… the opposite."

Okay. Okay. Breathe.

Every cell in my body screams for me to shut my mouth and run, but I clench my fists and will the words out. Going back is impossible, all I can do is go forwards.

"The doctors said I was a boy when I was born, for obvious reasons, and since then we've all gone along with it. But that's at least partially not true. I've known this, in one way or another, for a really long time, and soon how I feel on the inside will match the outside."

And there it is. My grip loosens and my back slumps.

"Oh," Eric says. His face softens and now *he* looks away. There's a quiet moment. I give him time to process while I watch, a thread of curiosity weaving into the noisy tapestry inside me as he removes his glasses. "So you're getting a sex change?" he says.

"I guess," I say, slowly so I don't panic again, "I can't really answer that unless I know what you think a sex change *is*."

"You *know*…" he says. His cheeks flush and he makes a snipping motion with his fingers.

I swallow and place my hands over my crotch, almost on instinct. Even if I was a fan of what I have down there, the idea of Eric thinking about my body that way, *talking* about my body that way, makes me squirm. I'm not a medical problem or a bunch of stitched-together parts, I'm a person. "I don't know? It's expensive. And so you know, they don't…" I mimic his snipping motion and his cheeks darken further. "It's more complicated than that. But I don't even know if that's the important part to me."

He bites his lip and rubs his knuckles. For some reason his embarrassment emboldens me. He's in unfamiliar territory too. I scoot a few inches closer to him, bunching his navy comforter between us.

"Listen," he says, "will you tell me if I cross a line?"

"It means a lot that you even asked that," I say, and now that I've said a few things, the words come easier. I brush my bangs out of my eyes and glance at the crack in his blinds, the huddled black sparrows arrayed on the power lines. The oak tree that's been here longer than any of us. "To be honest I don't know where the line *is*. But," I say. "Yeah. Don't worry. It's…you understand how hard this is for me, right?"

He nods. "I think I've been waiting for you to say something for a long time…"

"Longer than you probably know." I allow myself to breathe. "If you ask something I don't wanna answer, I'll tell you. And like I was saying, surgery is expensive and… whatever. For now my plan is to start taking hormones, have the little bit of facial hair I've got removed, get my name changed, and see how I feel."

262

"What will the hormones do?" he says, and now there's a naked, innocent curiosity in his eyes.

"It varies," I say. My face feels hot and I realize I'm mumbling. More talking about my body. I wonder if being trans will mean talking about my body for the rest of my life. "From person to person. Less body hair. Softer skin. My hair won't fall out like Dad's. Uh. You know. Fat distribution. Thighs…boobs…" I let my hair fall in front of my eyes again and rub my arm. "Probably I'll get plastic surgery for my face before I worry about things people can't see."

I'm so glad I can't see him. I can only imagine the look of disgust on his face. Right? I'm disgusted with myself. He must be disgusted with me too.

"I want to be pretty," I say, in a voice so small I can barely hear it. I clear my throat and say it again. "You don't have to be pretty to be a girl, but I still *want* to be."

"You *are* pretty though," he says, matter of fact, as if I'd gotten the weather wrong.

"What?" I part my hair from my eyes and look up, and it feels like the room is suddenly hot and quiet and full of something I can't quite name. Eric sits at the end of the bed, his legs tucked under him, folding and unfolding his glasses as he stares at me.

"You're pretty," he says again. His mouth tugs into a smile. "You've always been pretty." He knuckles his temple and shakes his head. "Maybe I always knew without

263

knowing." He bites the corner of his lip again and looks down at my legs. "I think I did. I think more than how you looked… We've always been… I don't know, it sounds stupid, but maybe I could feel it even when I couldn't see it. Like when I kissed you…you felt like a girl to me."

"I wish you wouldn't say that," I say. My throat clenches up and I feel my eyes burning.

"Why not?" he says. He sets his glasses aside and leans forward. "You're crying. I made you cry. God, I'm sorry…"

"I'm not stupid, okay?" I say. "I know what the world's like for people like me. Even if I am pretty, which I'm not, even if I win the genetic fucking lottery, I know what it's like."

"What's it like, Morgan?" Eric says. "I don't understand."

I look down at his carpet with burning eyes, remembering a lifetime of rough-housing, of building Lego, of looking up at the stars glued to the ceiling, of talking about little-kid bullshit like it was the most important thing in the whole world. I swallow hard. "I don't know if anyone will love me the way that I really am. The time you kissed me might be the last time anyone ever does, and even then you had to have your glasses off. You said so yourself. So I appreciate what you're trying to do, but you don't have to. I've come to terms with that."

My shoulders shake and my mouth twists, but I don't let myself cry. I close my eyes and hear him shift next to me. It's okay, I tell myself. It's only natural for him to pull away.

Something touches my chin and gently tilts it up. I open my eyes to find Eric wearing his glasses again, his expression open and warm, with a hint of a smile. He turns my face towards his. His thumb reaches up to swipe a tear from my cheek. I feel my lips part. I feel like I should say something, but then he leans in and his breath is on my chin and neck and then his lips are on mine.

He tastes, of all things, like chocolate cake.

ERIC

I lace my fingers in hers and hold her hand, gently but firmly.

Her hand, I think, as our lips dance at their intersection. She doesn't pull away this time. She. Now that I know, how could it have been different? I slip my tongue where her lips part, and as I rise to my knees I graze my fingers down her jaw, her neck. She shudders. Her fingers close around my hand like she's drowning and a wordless sound escapes her mouth into mine. She dips her face to the side and slips her hand free. It rests on my neck, smooth and warm, and her shaking lips hover near my ear.

"You don't have to do this," she whispers.

I kiss her temple, her cheekbone. I run my hand under her hoodie, up her smooth, flat stomach. She sighs again and I smile.

"I do," I say.

She pulls my face to hers and kisses me three, four, five times.

"Of course I have to," I say.

She looks down, a hint of sadness creeping into her eyes even as her skin flushes under my hand.

"What's wrong?" I say, worried I've gone too far. "Do you want to stop?"

"It's hard not to feel like a boy," she says. Her voice cracks. She shakes her head.

And, I mean, I'm not blind. All I know is that I've never felt like this before, that under the things about her body she might not like, she *is* a girl, vibrating the same hue as any other. And she's more than any girl, any friend, any girlfriend. She's Morgan. My Morgan.

"But…" she says. Her eyes bore into me, and I realize the first song I ever write is going to be about her. Morgan Gardner deserves a song. "My chest is flat. My shoulders are broad. I've got a…you know… how could you possibly…"

"Some girls are tall," I say. I kiss her forehead. "Some girls have broad shoulders." I kiss the bridge of her nose. "Some girls have flat chests." I kiss her chin and let my breath flow down her neck. "And I guess I never thought about it before, but if you're a girl, then some girls have whatever you have." I kiss her collarbone.

Her head tilts back and her fingers twist through my hair. I plant kiss after kiss on her neck.

"Just don't touch my chest," she says. "Or *there*. Okay?"

"Okay."

My phone buzzes. I ignore it and it *keeps* buzzing, but nothing can take my attention from this moment. Morgan plants a hand on my chest and pushes me back, back, back, until I'm lying down with her poised above. She cups my face in both hands and kisses me like I've never been kissed, like each of us was a key built for the other and now, after seventeen years, both of us have been unlocked. We kiss until my lips feel numb. Her hair gets in the way and my glasses bump her nose. I consider taking them off, but I want her to know I see her.

She *deserves* to be seen.

"Eric..." she says. She lays her body across mine and ranges her hands across me, bicep to belt, her fingers pinpoints of light. Her words come in the gaps between kisses, desperate and quick.

"Yeah?"

"Eric."

"Morgan."

She pushes herself up and stares down at me, her dark eyes glimmering, her face framed by falling hair.

"Eric," she says. She lifts my hand and kisses the knuckle, letting her eyes close again. "You don't have to say anything. I don't...I don't want to pressure you or anything. Because this is crazy, right?" Her thumb traces the lines in my palm and she takes a breath, still shaky. "But, I think I—"

"God *fucking* damn it, Eric! When you don't answer the phone your mother gets on *my* ass. Call her back *now* or—"

Dad's voice explodes between us as the door flies open. Morgan screams and scrambles back, adjusting her clothes. I sit up and pull my shirt down to cover my stomach, hot adrenaline pumping all my pleasure away. Dad stomps into the room, lost in his own anger for *just* a moment before he pauses, eyes wide.

Maybe we separated in time. I try to swallow the dryness in my throat and glance at Morgan with a sinking dread. Her hair is a wild mess. Her clothes are wrinkled and sitting askew on her shoulders and hips. Her cheeks are flushed, her lips are pink, and a splotch is already forming on her neck. She looks at me with eyes drenched in panic and my gut twists as I search for a way to make this not be happening and come up blank.

"Dad," I say. "What happened to knocking?"

"Out," Dad says. His voice rumbles like an island boiling up from the sea. "Get the fuck *out* of my *house*."

"Carson," Morgan says. She holds her arms around herself and glares at him. I know that look from a dozen scenes of bullies biting off more than they can chew, a dozen suicidal scraps started when she was immolating herself. I imagine this is what it feels like when a soldier sees a grenade roll next to him with no time to dive away. "Listen—"

"I've always known you were a freak," he says. "And now you've corrupted my son." He snaps his arm towards the hall and points. "Get. Out."

"You don't know anything about me, actually," she says, her voice dripping with venom. "And you're welcome to fuck yourself." She starts to get up, her slender hands balled into fists. Dad won't let her leave now. I've seen him fight so much with Peyton and Mom over the years that I know how this goes, but I'm too slow.

He stomps across the room, all two hundred and thirty pounds of him, takes the front of Morgan's hoodie in his fist, and shoves all one hundred and twenty pounds of her back onto the bed. She sprawls back, her dark eyes smoking with fury, and as surely as the sun rises I know she's about to lunge at him.

I move, clutching Dad's shoulder, turning him, and pushing him into the wall – he's got forty pounds on me, but I'm younger, faster, and in better shape. Morgan scrambles to her feet and stands behind me in the moment it takes Dad to come to terms with the new shape of things.

"*Don't,*" I say. I start to say, "Don't touch *her*," but a reflex stops me. He'll laugh at her and besides, Morgan clearly doesn't want people like him to know yet. I choke down the rest, grind my teeth, and glare at him while he fumes.

"So," Dad says. "Turns out it's you."

I let go of him and take a step back, staying on the balls of my feet in case he tries anything.

"Three sons," he says. "Inevitable one'd take a swing."

"Fuck off, Dad."

The back of his hand cracks across my face faster than I can see. Pain spreads in purple ripples across my jaw and my vision swims as I stumble to the bed, his shadow spreading over me like ink. I hear Morgan yell and take a step but I reach out, pressing a hand into her stomach, and thank god she stops.

"I gave you life," Dad says. "I paid for this house. I pay for your food. I've given you *everything* you have. I'll treat you however I *want*, boy. I *should* have knocked some sense into you years ago." He turns on Morgan, spit flying from his lips. "And you! You took my son from me, faggot."

"Me?" Morgan says. Her voice breaks. "What? You think you're father of the fucking year?"

I stand, remaining between them, and rub my jaw only to discover tears on my cheek.

"Get out. Of my house. Don't come back. And if I find out you've so much as *looked* at my son, I'll make life hell for you *and* your trailer trash daddy."

"Come on, Eric," Morgan says. She touches my shoulder and turns me so I can see the pleading look in her eyes. "Let's go."

"Do it," Dad says. "Go ahead and make my fucking

271

day." His sulphur gaze turns to Morgan. "Now. I thought I told you to leave."

Morgan pulls me and I follow her a few steps, but then dig my heels into the carpet. Should I really leave? What should I do? Where would I go?

"I won't leave without you," she says.

I squeeze her hand.

She squeezes back.

"Okay," I say, and take a step towards her.

"Now hold on," Dad says.

"You heard Morgan," I say. She pulls me towards the hall and I look over my shoulder. "Go fuck yourself!"

"Come back here!" Dad yells. He lurches towards us, but we're both faster than him. We scramble for the stairs and then out the door, hand in hand, invincible as long as we're together. I throw myself into her car while she starts the engine and we're out of the driveway just in time to see Dad explode out the front door and onto the lawn.

I know I'm going to pay for this later. But right now, with my heart hammering in my ears, it's worth it. I lean out the window, hold out both middle fingers, and as we careen out of the neighbourhood Morgan's laughter is the most beautiful music I've ever heard.

MORGAN

I stop at the gas station at the bottom of the hill and I kiss him while the engine idles. I'm not scared any more, and I'm not shy. My fingers are in his curls as I pull him to me, as we navigate the tiny space, and I didn't know kissing could feel like this.

Eric makes a deep, satisfied sound, only to have it cut short with a wince. I pull back and see how one side of his face is starting to swell. I hold his hand, and I kiss his jaw, and I head inside for two cans of Coke. When I return the car is quiet, but Eric is smiling down at something on his phone.

"Here," I say. I hand him the Cokes as we hit the road again. "Drink one, hold the other against your jaw. We can get you some ice later."

"I'll be fine," he says. "Thanks." He taps a beat on one of the cans and bites his lip. "Should we...talk? About this?"

"I'm scared," I say. I look at him and in the very last dark rays of the setting sun he's as beautiful as he's always been. "I don't know. This is all happening so fast."

"I think it's been happening for years," he says. He flashes me a smile only to wince when the Coke can touches his skin.

"But what do we do now?" I say as I turn onto Lafayette Street, distantly aware I'm driving on autopilot towards Federal Park. "You can't go home, but if you stay with us, your dad'll—"

"I love you," Eric says. I favour him with another glance and he grins sheepishly. "I love you."

"I love you too," I whisper.

We pull into the parking lot and I run my hands over the steering wheel, touching the smooth spots worn down by Mom's hands and noticing how my own fingers fit into the grooves. The night sounds kick up, the frogs, and crickets, and a few late-season cicadas. And I just told Eric that I love him.

Eric hops out of the car and I follow. "I want to show you something," he says over his shoulder. We walk deeper into the park. Soon the lights from the parking lot fade to nothing and all we're left with is moonlight. We cross a clearing where we used to lie out sometimes watching clouds and, eventually, he stops in front of an old, old maple tree swaying in the breeze. "Here it is."

"A tree?" I stand beside him and take his hand without

thinking, and as my neck cranes up I realize there are dozens of fireflies flitting back and forth within its branches, and it feels familiar somehow.

"This is where I started to fall in love with you," he says.

"What?"

He sits in the grass, gently pulling me down into his lap. I've never sat in a boy's lap before, hardly dreamed I could, and I suddenly realize I've lost more muscle than I thought, or he's gotten even bigger in the last year. I feel so small as I tuck my legs to the side and he winds his arm around me. I rest my cheek in his hair and close my eyes. His hand rubs up and down my side.

"We were twelve," he says in a voice as soft as the wind in the grass. "Eleven? That part's hard to remember. It was a long time ago. But I remember you were climbing this tree. I was standing down here, so worried that you'd climbed too high. High enough I could barely see. You fell, and for a minute I thought you'd died, and if you were dead, then I wanted to die too."

"Always a drama queen," I whisper just above his ear. The wind mixes with my voice and in this boy's lap, my boy's lap, I feel close to whole.

"It was a long fall." He laughs despite everything. His fingers dig into my side and I arch my back and squeal, but he holds me close before I can get away in earnest. "I was hovering over you, trying to see if you were breathing. You opened your eyes, and I don't know. The light caught them just right. Your hair was getting long and it had fanned out around you." He kisses my collarbone, the side of my neck, the joint between my ear and my jaw. I tilt my face up to the moon, my stomach a heated tangle of too many emotions. "You were beautiful. I loved you already then. I didn't know it, and I didn't know I was waiting for you to tell me who you are, but both are true."

I kiss his forehead. He kisses my temple. We lie in the grass, kissing gently to keep from hurting where his father struck him, touching where it's safe to touch between the minefield of my body and the weight of years. The mountains sing around us. Who knows how long? Eventually I'm lying with my head on his shoulder, curled next to him, eyes closed and perfectly ready to fall asleep in the grass, and I wish I could, I wish we could, but one thought won't leave me.

"Eric?"

"Mm?"

"What're we gonna do?"

"No idea," he says, but the reality hangs between us: his father, what's at stake for both of us. "What's the worst that could happen?"

I can think of a lot, but I don't say it.

"But we're going to be together," he says. "No matter what."

"Okay, Eric," I say. I nuzzle in closer to him and breathe in deep.

There's a long pause between us before Eric starts to speak again, his voice soft, like he's telling me a fairy tale. "We're thirty," he says. "We've got an apartment in Los Angeles, maybe a duplex. Three bedrooms so your dad can retire and come live with us. The third is, I don't know, maybe an office, maybe it's got a race car bed in it."

I hold in a laugh and let him spin a fantasy, like I've done so many times on my own.

"I'm in a band, maybe doing some session recording on the side. You've got a job freelancing, some arcane video editing thing I'll never understand. We've got a lot of books. Maybe a dog."

"Blue pointer," I say sleepily. "I want a blue pointer."

"We've got a blue pointer," he says, stretching and nodding slowly. "Named Elvis. And we're married."

"What?"

"I'm being stupid," Eric says. "I'm sorry. I'm rushing things."

"No," I say. "No. No, it's nice."

"Something to think about," he says.

"Mm-hmm," I say. And I do think about it as I drift down to sleep.

Eventually, he wakes me up, and we shuffle back to the car together, arm in arm, our birthday hours long behind us.

EIGHTEENTH BIRTHDAY

MORGAN

My new iPhone chirps out the sound I've set for my work email. I hold a dress to my face and groan. Jasmine looks up from rummaging in my closet, all part of her self-appointed duty as birthday outfit coordinator, and rolls her eyes.

"Don't check it," she says.

"I won't," I say. I nod and stuff what *I* think is the best of my five black dresses into the open suitcase on my bed and then stand there, jiggling my hands, staring at the little black rectangle on my night stand. "But I should."

"You *shouldn't*," Jasmine replies. She throws me a pair of sandals I'd thought I wouldn't need until spring, but considering I'm headed to Miami, it makes sense. I'm surprising Eric for his eighteenth birthday – our eighteenth birthday – with a trip down to Florida.

After the fight with Carson, we both knew Eric couldn't stay in Thebes. His mom, Peyton and Chelsea rented a house together in Miami with a spare room for Eric. Then, over Christmas break, Jenny came to our trailer in her minivan to pick up Eric. Instead of it being awkward, like I'd feared, Jenny said that she was happy for me, that I looked so much like my mom it hurt her heart. Eric left with only a suitcase and his guitar. Watching him climb into the van and disappear down the highway was one of the hardest things I've ever done.

Since then, we've had phone calls, Skype chats that have lasted late into the night, and even care packages, full of everything from baked goods to T-shirts, so we don't forget how the person we love smells.

Sometimes I like to dance through the house when I'm alone, wearing Eric's oversized Joy Division shirt, while one of his playlists blares through the trailer. Being apart from him this long has been agony, like one of my own limbs has fallen asleep and won't wake up, but I try to focus on how much better our reunion will be because of this.

Me and Dad decided together over the summer, after a kind of awkward acknowledgement that hormones were already having their, ahem, desired effect, that public school in Thebes might not be the safest place for me. I'd improved my grades enough to qualify for more advanced courses so at least I had a way out. Roane State Community

College offered online classes for everything I needed, and the looser schedule left me more time to work on video editing and vlogging. The latter started as a personal video journal to record the first days and years of my life lived fully as a girl, or now a woman I guess, but then someone randomly found the first few vlogs I'd uploaded, liked them, shared them, and now I have five thousand subscribers and around a million views each time I upload a Sunday video. Who knew audiences were so hungry for the life of a trans girl from Nowhere, Tennessee?

Between ad revenue and editing work, I'm making a little money – enough to pay for hormones, clothes and this trip, and I'm proud of that. The thing is, though, it's about more than the work, and it's about more than money, which is why I'm still tempted to check my phone. Every so often, I get a message from a trans kid my age or younger. Sometimes they try to hide how desperate and afraid they are, sometimes they're open about how they can't imagine a way out of their lives. Some of them live as close as Georgia, others as far away as Argentina or Korea. Almost universally they live in small towns, like Thebes. They don't have dads like mine, still uncomfortable at times, but glad I'm alive, and they don't have friends like Jasmine, and they don't have anything *close* to Eric.

"You ready?" Dad asks as he emerges from his bedroom. I nod, hug Jasmine goodbye, and we load into the car in silence as tendrils of fog drag down from the mountains, chilling my bare arms and legs until the first licks of sunlight infuse me with warmth. Jasmine waves from her car as we pull away from the trailer.

The drive is silent until we're out of Thebes proper, and I'm glad for it because there's too much going on inside me. As we turn onto the interstate headed west for Nashville, I think, *someday when I come back here I won't be coming home.*

It's a sobering thought. As much as I hate Thebes, the idea of leaving for ever makes me feel like I'm at the top of a roller coaster. Because if *this* isn't my home, what is? The furthest I've ever been from my hometown is a few miles into Kentucky and Georgia. But then I remember that Eric is my home. *For ever*, because he promised. *We* promised.

But…what if I show up at his doorstep and something has changed? I look at myself in the passenger-side mirror and my stomach tightens. My face has rounded out a little, my skin is smoother. I used some of my YouTube money to pay for laser hair removal, and I've been using voice tutorials I found online, but it's still early days. Eric says I'm beautiful, but he's only seen me in carefully posed selfies, on grainy webcams, or in videos where everything is lit and filtered and edited.

"You got your driver's licence, right?" Dad asks for possibly the seventh time in the last twenty-four hours.

"Yeah, Dad."

"And your name-change papers in case they give you trouble?"

"Yeah." Hard to imagine why they even would when all I changed was my middle name.

"And you printed your boarding pass?" he says.

"*Yeah*, Dad," I say. I roll my eyes and show him the folded piece of paper in my purse.

"Okay," he says. "All right. All right. I'll shut up."

"You don't have to shut up," I say softly as we climb higher and higher up Cumberland Plateau, sheer mountain walls rising up to our left to partially blot out the sun. "I didn't *say* shut up."

"Better not," he says with a weak smile.

"But could you please stop babying me?" I say. "Please? I *am* eighteen."

"Emphasis on the *teen*," he mutters.

"*Dad!*"

"Okay!" he says. He holds up both hands long enough to show he's giving up, before placing them back on the wheel. "All grown up. Nothing left to learn. You got it, bud." I try to hide how much I tense at being called "bud", but either I do a bad job, or Dad's become tuned-in enough to see that I hate it. He winces and rubs his forehead. "Sorry. Sorry…"

"It's fine," I say. I put on one of Eric's playlists and silently turn my attention to the valley below as John Denver croons, appropriately enough, about country roads. I know Dad's doing his best. I know I'm *insanely* lucky, especially now that I have some other trans kids' stories to compare mine to. And I know Dad gets worried, but things feel different for me now. Used to be, even when I was swinging at other people, I really only hated myself.

Now – when someone yells something cruel from a car, or treats my body like an inconvenience or a freak show, I don't really get mad at myself. Now, I get mad at *them*. I can throw a half-finished drink at a car full of catcallers. I can commiserate with other trans people on forums about how much flying sucks. Now that I'm eighteen, I can vote out politicians who try to pass bad laws. It's productive anger.

Dad turns the volume down as we crest a rise and start drifting down a winding mountain road. "Morgan?"

"Yes, Dad?" I roll my eyes again reflexively and immediately feel guilty.

"I just need you to know that I love you," he says.

"Love you too," I say.

He takes my hand in his, rests both on the gear shift, and squeezes.

"But I reserve the right to be annoying."

I throw my head back and groan, but my smile widens. "Thanks, Dad. I'll remember that."

Before I know it, we're pulling into Nashville International Airport. As we unload my bag and suitcase

I can't help noticing the stiffness in Dad's shoulders. And then there we are, a father and daughter facing each other on a raised ribbon of concrete, jets screaming overhead, the wind whipping my hair while he blinks faster and faster.

"So hey," I say. I favour him with a grin. "You know that I'm coming back, right? This is just for a few days? And when I do move out, I'm still gonna come back and visit all the time."

He nods and pulls me into a hug that neither of us breaks for a long time. When we finally part he rummages in his pocket and produces an envelope with Mom's handwriting on it. "This is the last one. Thought it might be nice if she kept you company on the plane."

"Thank you," I say, "for holding on to all of these." I tuck the letter into my coat pocket, close to my heart.

"She'd be so proud of you."

I nod and now it's my turn to hold back tears. We hug one more time, and Dad gets back in his car without ever taking his eyes off me. I take a breath, and then a step, and then I'm through the automatic doors and one with the crowd.

ERIC

A breeze blows in from the ocean. I can faintly hear dogs barking and the rumble of car stereos. Mom sings from the kitchen as I tune my guitar. I lie back on Peyton and Chelsea's couch, *our* couch, I guess, at once gross because it smells like cigarettes and spilled beer but somehow more comfortable than anything from our old house. It had been weird to see how run-down this place was, but even more surprising was the fact that Mom was fine with it.

"Never cared much about all that," Mom said when I asked her about it. We sat on the porch, me practising guitar in a hammock while she smiled and waved to the neighbours. "Appearances and all. I came up on a holler in Pikeville, barefoot for the most part. Your father cared about appearances, and it seemed right to make myself useful."

She leaned back so she was directly in the sun and

stretched like a cat, and I was amazed how she seemed to be growing younger. "The way *I* see it, the place where you are doesn't matter as much as the *person* you are and the people you're with." She smiled at me, and even months in, it was electric to see her smile this much. "My sons are happy and healthy. We've got enough food. I like my sons' girlfriends. My job's tolerable. Our air-conditioning works sometimes. What more could a woman really ask for?"

"You really like Morgan?" I said.

"Oh, of course." She sighed and folded her hands over her chest. "I've always loved Morgan. Nothing could change that."

Mom's made it clear the last few days that she didn't want me to go anywhere tonight, which seemed kind of unnecessary since it's a week night and, for the first time in a long time, I actually care about my schoolwork. Maybe I never realized how much slack teachers gave me while I was on the football team. Maybe it's knowing I sink or swim on nothing but my own merit now that I'm out of high school and away from Dad's money. Maybe seeing how hard other students have it at Miami Dade College has finally made me respect all my advantages.

Either way, between practising guitar, homework and talking to Morgan, my evenings are almost completely accounted for. I miss her, and it seems wrong not to be with her on our birthday, but I've told myself it's only one year.

"Here you go, man," Peyton says. I rise up from my thoughts to find him standing over me, a Florida ID card held between his fingers. He flips it towards me and I just barely catch it before it falls through the strings into the belly of my guitar. Closer investigation reveals my picture, my name, *all* the normal details, except the birth date is three years older than it should be. I stuff the ID in my pocket before Mom can come out of the kitchen and see it.

Peyton grins. "Happy birthday, good luck at Churchill's, and if you get caught I don't know you."

"Got it," I say. "Thanks, man." The song I'm writing is almost done, and now I get to play it at the open mic at one of the coolest bars in Miami. Excitement runs through me.

"No problem," Peyton says. He sniffs the air and leans towards the kitchen. "That smells amazing! How long till it's ready?"

Mom emerges from the kitchen, wiping sweat from her temples with a smile, and I can't help noticing as she slides her phone into her back pocket. Was she texting someone? "Soon. Peyton, could you run to the corner store for soda?" He flips his keys around his fingers and heads out. She leans against the couch, that smile only widening, a mischievous twinkle in her eye. "So! Eighteen!"

"Yup," I say.

"How do you feel?"

"I don't know," I say. I drop my hands in my lap and roll my head back. "I don't smoke, it's not an election year, and I've still got to go to school tomorrow, so it sort of doesn't feel like anything."

"You're not sad we're not throwing you a party?" Mom says, and you'd think she would sound regretful, but the corners of her mouth are twitching and that playful air is still there. Obviously she's planning something, *has* been planning something for a little while, but for the life of me I can't figure out what it might be.

"I'm happy just to be here," I say. I pull her into a hug and kiss her cheek, then grab my guitar by the neck and head outside, where I flop into the hammock. There are no stars in the city, but I stare up into the blue smear where they would be and let my eyes follow the planes blinking red and blue as they soar overhead, imagining all the lives and all the connections on each one, and suddenly the last few notes fall into place.

MORGAN

The woman at the flight bridge smiles and says, "Have a nice flight, miss," and that makes me feel good. The elderly woman who takes the aisle seat next to me smiles too. She pats my arm, calls me "dearie", and tells me shakily that this is her first flight as well. Never thought she *would* fly, but she's a great-grandma as of yesterday and no way is she not going to hold that child.

I try to focus on her but the plane is in position now, engines revving for take-off, and my eyes keep darting to the window. I've always loved roller coasters, so I *thought* I would be fine, but suddenly my stomach is trying to crawl out through my mouth.

"Yes, ma'am, a sweet little great-granddaughter," she says with a proud beam. I blink and forget where I am for a moment. I've been called "miss" and "young lady" and "young woman" and "sweetie" and words for women I don't like thinking about, but never "ma'am" until now. One day, I realize, all these things about my gender will probably just feel normal, and that's something to look forward to.

I slip my hand in my pocket, fingering the edge of the letter like a talisman as the plane starts to rise. I take out the envelope and open it slowly, partially because my hands are suddenly shaking and partially because this, the very last of Mom's letters, feels like something worth savouring. But eventually the anticipation ends and there's nothing left but to take the final step.

Morgan,

Happy eighteenth birthday, my love.

I've been a bit selfish, leaving you these little time bombs. The thing is, the scariest part of dying isn't what might happen to me when I'm gone – I don't know what I believe, except that the universe is fundamentally good under all the hurt and misunderstanding, and there must be more to all of us than our flesh and blood. No.

What keeps me up at night, and what has pushed me to leave you these yearly reminders, is a simple fear of being left behind. Imagine those nights, as I'm sure you've had by now, when you find out your friends have gone out without you, or kept some important part of their life from you. Now multiply that as much as you care to. It hurts, the idea that life can go on without you, that all the private mysteries will keep growing like gardens behind an iron wall, especially when the lives in question are the people most important to you. Not that you or your father would ever forget me, of course! I don't doubt that for a second. But…I don't know. I'm at a loss for words. You must remember how rare that is for me.

Listen. No more presents or surprises. You've grown too far past the child I know for me to guess what you might want. All I have is this, and these will be my last words to you:

Wherever I am, whatever else I'm doing, you're in my thoughts. Always. Whatever seeds you plant will have my eye on them. Whatever plans you make I'll cheer for you. Whatever kind of person you become, no matter how different from my daydreams, I will treasure you. No matter how lonely you ever have felt, I've been there, and no matter how dark things may get as you grow older, I'll be there as well. You are my favourite person in the world and the thing I am proudest of.

Love you for ever,
Mom

I hold the letter to my chest and lean against the window. Far below us Nashville disappears, until all I can see are suburbs and the rolling green mountains. Then we're in the clouds and I wonder if she's watching me right now, if it really is *that* cliché and heaven is an invisible kingdom in the sky.

I press a hand to the window and imagine Mom's hand pressed to the other side, her in a white robe with wings and a halo giving me a corny thumbs-up, wishing me luck and whispering her approval of Eric. It's stupid but it's also comforting.

More likely, and more complicated, is the thought that she's just gone, and that this letter is the last part of her I'll ever see or touch, and the only afterlife she or anyone ever gets is the ripples their lives make in the world around them – heaven in the hearts of those who live on, love branching out like roots in an old-growth forest.

The ground finally disappears completely behind the clouds. I close my eyes and count down the hours until I can tell all of this to the boy I love, the boy who's waiting for me in paradise.

ERIC

I stop playing guitar for a moment to jot down lyrics and tabs in my pocket notebook, and I'm so absorbed in making sure everything's just right that I barely register the sound of brakes squeaking at the edge of the yard.

It's a busy neighbourhood, with neighbours constantly changing, so at least once a week some new person drops by to see if an old friend or relative still lives at this address. I swing in the breeze and scribble away, tongue poking from the side of my mouth.

But then a familiar voice hits me. I sit up so fast the hammock shoots out from under me and I tumble onto the porch, just barely managing not to smash my guitar.

"Here," she says, and I'm certain it's her voice, but is it? It's changed so much from how it was, and I've only heard it through phones and computer speakers.

I clamber to my feet and just make out a taxi rumbling at the edge of the driveway. Two silhouettes rummage in the open trunk. They pull out a suitcase and a backpack and the smaller of the two figures takes both. I try and remember to breathe.

"Okay. Yeah, I've got it from here. Thanks again."

She grunts as she lifts the suitcase and in a few small steps she's within the light cast from our porch, this girl from the taxi.

And it's her.

She's here.

No satellites pulling her into pixels, but *here* in the fluttering light, her dark hair spilling over her shoulders, her eyes glittering midnight lakes, her body in a *Brides of Dracula* tank top and denim jean shorts. She's transformed completely through a million subtle softenings and yet she's still herself, *more* herself than she ever was before.

She looks up. She smiles.

"Hi," she says in that voice. Its newness mingles with its familiarity, and it's like Romeo falling for Juliet all at once and, all the same, like Odysseus finally hearing his wife again after years and miles apart. In a second, I'm vaulting over the porch railing, stumbling, and then running for her with none of the grace or skill football ever taught me.

She drops her bags just in time for me to sweep her into my arms, and for a moment I'm holding her so tight she can't even move her arms to hold me back. "Breathe. Can't breathe."

I unwind my arms and she laughs. My hands cup her chin and tilt her face up to mine, and I think I might ask how she got here, or how she hid this from me, but then she rises to her toes and all I can do is kiss her.

She hops up and wraps her legs around my waist, hooks her arms around my neck, and I hold the girl I love suspended in the air. I take in her smell through the humid air and run my hands over as much of her back as I can reach. This could go on for ever and I'd certainly die happy, but eventually she lolls her head back, her black hair blending into the night as a breeze from the ocean kicks it into motion. I let her down and she leans against me, looking up through her eyelashes, her fingers curling against my chest as we catch our breath.

"Surprise." Morgan brushes her bangs from her eyes and laughs. "Happy birthday, Eric."

"Happy birthday, Morgan."

MORGAN

He sings about Tennessee snow and a girl locked in a cage with bars made of fire. I curl my body around his back and stare up at him. The covers are a knotted mess. The fitted sheet is loose and bunched. The vibrations from his singing echo from his back into my stomach. Eric said that tomorrow night I can listen to him play the songs onstage at one of the best bars in the city. Just thinking about watching him play for a crowd feels so close to my dreams that my breath catches.

He sings about poison mountains and roads like typewriter ribbons waiting to spool, about kisses in the street and heartbreak in hiding. I close my eyes and let my mind wander. His voice lifts me up, the lyrics melting together.

But then he sings about a dark-eyed girl full of secrets and an empty-headed boy tumbling down from the sky, and how the girl filled her cold spots with fire, cooling the boy enough for him to see. The idea that I could fit into any of these flowery metaphors makes me want to cover my face with a pillow. But if that's how he sees me then I certainly won't rush to correct him. His voice rings earnest and clear and I can almost believe in this version of myself.

The song winds to a close. He sets his guitar aside and makes a nervous little face. I rest my head in his lap and smile up at him and tell him the song was as beautiful as him. We kiss, and we kiss, and we kiss, our whole future spiralling before us.

IF YOU HAVE BEEN AFFECTED
BY THE ISSUES RAISED IN THIS BOOK,
THE FOLLOWING ORGANISATIONS
CAN HELP.

Samaritans are available round the clock,
every single day of the year.

Talk to us any time you like in your own way and
off the record, about whatever's getting to you.

Call us free any time on 116 123
Or email jo@samaritans.org
Visit us: find your nearest branch on
samaritans.org

Family and individual support for teenagers and children with gender identity issues

Mermaids supports children and young people up to 19 years old suffering from gender identity issues, and their families and supporting professionals. Our resources provide a vital lifeline for young people and families who are searching for support and information.

www.mermaidsuk.org.uk

Helpline:
0808 801 0400
Open Monday – Friday; 9am – 9pm
(Bank Holiday opening times may vary)

info@mermaidsuk.org.uk

ACKNOWLEDGEMENTS

Everyone warns you about the second book, and it turns out it's all true. The novel you just read would absolutely not have entered the world without a network of professional and emotional support for which I am eternally grateful. In no particular order, here are the people I need to thank.

Joelle Hobeika, you opened the door to this crazy job, and I'll never forget our first conversation when I was a sophomore in college. Sara Shandler and Hayley Wagreich, you have been absolute saints through my habit of stumbling over deadlines, and without your reassurances I might have given up before we landed on a book worth really being proud of. Thank you to Sarah Barley and everyone at Flatiron for believing in this project and for your patience and support. And thank you to all of the above for being willing to put up with me over drinks and too-long phone calls. I consider you friends as much as editors, and I hope the feeling is mutual.

Writing is lonely work, and writing while living with mental illness is even lonelier. The following people regularly went out of their way to get me out of the house these last two years. Anthony, Sierra, Amanda and Luna: I don't know where I would have been without our Saturday night ritual. There were weeks when making a meal, playing D&D, and watching a movie were the only things I looked forward to. The tradition itself might be over, but I still cherish all the time each of you chooses to spend with me. Kayla and Claudio: one for being among my most ferocious advocates, the other for being so clearly gentle and unambiguously decent that you were the first Chattanoogan I came out to in real life.

Special thanks as well to Kyle and Athena. You both live too far away to get me out of the house, but your writing advice and friendship have meant more to me than I quite know how to say. As we three grow older and more young trans people emerge, it's good to know I'll always have y'all to keep me company while we grow into our roles as the trans aunties and uncles (and eventually grandmothers and grandfathers, ugh!) that we never got to have.

Finally, thank you to my parents, Karol and Toby, and my sister, Katie, for your unfailing love and support. I doubt I would have lived to witness the publication of this book without you. You are a better family than most trans people even know to ask for, and I don't want you to think for a moment that I don't know how blessed I am.

MEREDITH RUSSO was born, raised and lives in Tennessee. She started living as her true self in late 2013 and has never looked back.

DISCUSSION QUESTIONS

- *Birthday* opens with Morgan and Eric at the water park, playing a game to see how long they can each hold their breath. This is also the first moment Morgan decides to tell Eric about her identity. What significance might the water park and holding your breath have in Morgan's journey to coming out of the closet? Why start here?

- We have a window into Morgan's and Eric's minds and how incredibly close their friendship is. In what ways do we feel this closeness and how their relationship has always been more than just a friendship?

- Early on, both Morgan and Eric wrestle with the posibility they might be gay. How are gender and sexuality different? Discuss how over the course of the novel their notions of gender and sexuality evolve as two very separate parts of an individual's identity.

- Early in the book, Peyton uses slurs and targets both Morgan and Eric for their relationship and identities. However, towards the end we see a change in his character. Discuss the underlying emotions and environment that caused him to lash out. Can a person really change and redeem themselves?

- In Morgan's mom's first tape to Morgan, she says, "You were such a wonderful child." How do the recurring birthday notes help Morgan see herself for who she truly is? What role do the parents in the story play in the development of Morgan's identity, insecurities and final confidence?

- Football plays a key role throughout the story, whether it concerns Morgan's relationship with her dad, her relationship with Eric, or her relationship with herself. Why is football so important in all of these instances? How does football serve as a symbol of gender and tradition when Morgan is growing and breaking out of stereotypes?

- When Eric kisses Morgan, she thinks, "This is how a kiss is supposed to make you feel." Jasmine kisses Morgan the same night that Eric kisses Morgan. Discuss the difference between these two moments and how each one uncovers something new about Morgan and Eric and how they relate to each other.

- After Morgan puts make-up on, she thinks, "And there she is." Talk about this statement. What about this moment is so significant to Morgan? How is finally seeing who she is reflected in the mirror both the climax of her life thus far and what spurs her to spiral into one of her darker moments?

- When Eric cuts his hair, Susan says, "You look so much better." What role does Susan play in Eric's character development? In what ways are Susan and Morgan different? How do these differences make Morgan a better match for Eric?

- "My body is a machine, and I'm in control." Discuss the intense turnaround we see in Morgan's personality and behaviour. How does this mirror the anger and violence we originally saw in Peyton? Why does Morgan want her body to be a machine? Can we ever really be totally in control? Discuss the difference between internal and external validation and what role these two things play in Morgan's life when she joins the football team.

- At different times throughout the book, both Morgan and Eric refer to Morgan as "sick" or "wrong". What do you think of this? How is Morgan's "sickness" more representative of her refusal to be who she is rather than her underlying identity being inherently wrong?

- Eric always has a sixth sense when it comes to Morgan, and he gets there just in time to save Morgan from committing suicide. Where do you think this sense comes from?

- We revisit both characters on their birthday, and the novel is titled *Birthday*. How is this an important symbol of their friendship, love, and coming of age?

- In the end, it's not just Morgan who finally gets to be herself. How do Eric's and Morgan's journeys to find their authentic selves mimic each other? How do they both find peace and learn to accept all the complexities of their own identities? What can we learn from them about ourselves?

IF YOU'VE LOVED BIRTHDAY, READ ON
FOR AN EXTRACT FROM

"IMPORTANT AND BRAVE. READ THIS WONDERFUL
BOOK. JUST READ IT" JENNIFER NIVEN
Author of *All the Bright Places*

IF I WAS

your

GIRL

by MEREDITH RUSSO

The bus smelled of mildew, machine oil and sweat. As the suburban Atlanta sprawl disappeared behind us, I tapped my foot on the floor and chewed a lock of my newly long hair. A nagging voice reminded me that I was only a half-hour from home, that if I got off at the next stop and walked back to Smyrna, by sunset I could be in the comfort of my own bedroom, the familiar smell of Mom's starchy cooking in the air. She would hug me and we would sit down and watch awful reality TV shows together and she would fall asleep halfway through, and then nothing would change.

But something had to change. Because I had changed.

As I stared out at the swiftly moving trees, my mind was in a mall bathroom back in the city, the images shifting and jumbling like a kaleidoscope: a girl from my school, her scream as she recognized me. Her father rushing in, his rough, swift hands on my neck and shoulders. My body hitting the ground.

"You okay?" a voice practically screamed in my ear.

I looked up to see a guy wearing earbuds, his chin resting on the back of the seat in front of me. He gave me a lopsided smile as he pulled out the headphones. "Sorry."

"It's fine," I said. He stared at me, drumming his fingers on the headrest. I felt like I should say something, but I didn't trust my voice not to give me away.

"Where you headed?" He draped himself across the back of his seat like a cat, his arms nearly grazing my shins.

I wished I could roll up into a tiny, armoured ball and hide in my luggage.

"Lambertville," I said quietly. "Up in Hecate County."

"I'm going to Knoxville," he said, before going on to talk about his band, Gnosis Crank. I realized he'd only asked about me as a formality so he could talk about himself, but I didn't mind; it meant I didn't have to say that much. He told me about playing their first paying gig at a bar in Five Points.

"Cool," I said.

"Most of our songs are online if you wanna check them out."

"I will."

"How'd you get that black eye, by the way?"

"I—"

"Was it your boyfriend?" he asked.

My cheeks burned. He scratched his chin. He assumed I had a boyfriend. He assumed I was a girl. Under different circumstances, that would have thrilled me.

"I fell down," I said.

His smile turned sad.

"That's what my mom used to tell the neighbours," he said. "She deserved better, and so do you."

"Okay," I said, nodding. Maybe he was right, but what I deserved and what I could expect from life were two different things. "Thank you."

"No problem," he said as he put his headphones back

in. He smiled and added, "Nice meeting you," way too loudly before returning to his seat.

As we headed north on I-75 I texted Mom, letting her know I was okay and halfway there. She wrote back that she loved me, though I could feel her worry through the phone. I imagined her in our house all alone, Carrie Underwood playing on loop while the ceiling fans whispered overhead. Her hands covered in flour folded on the table in front of her, too many biscuits in the oven because she was used to cooking for two. If I'd had the strength to be normal, I thought, or at least the strength to die, then everyone would have been happy.

"Next stop Lambertville," the bus driver called over the harsh, tinny intercom. Outside the windows, none of the scenery had changed. The mountains looked the same. The trees looked the same. We could have been anywhere in the South, which is to say, nowhere. It seemed like the sort of place where Dad would live.

My hands shook as the bus lurched to a stop. I was the only passenger who stood up. The musician looked up from his magazine and nodded while I gathered my things. An older man with leathery skin and a sweat-stained work shirt scanned me from my feet to my neck without making eye contact. I stared straight ahead and pretended not to notice.

The door rattled open and the bus let out a hiss. I closed my eyes, whispered a short prayer to a god I wasn't sure really listened any more, and stepped down. The sickly humid afternoon heat hit me like a solid wall.

It had been six years since I had seen my father. I had rehearsed this moment over and over in my head. I would run up and hug him, and he would kiss the top of my head, and for the first time in a long time, I would feel safe.

"That you?" Dad asked, his voice muffled by the bass rumble of the bus engine. I squinted against the harsh light. He wore a pair of wire-rim sunglasses, and his hair was at least half silver now. Deep lines had formed around his mouth. Mom called these "laugh lines", so I wasn't sure how he had got them. Only his mouth was as I remembered it: the same thin, horizontal slash.

"Hi, Dad," I said. The sunglasses made it easier to look him in the face. We both stood rooted in place.

"Hi," he said after a while. "Put your things in the back." He opened the back of the wagon and got in the car. I deposited my luggage and joined him. I remembered this car; it was at least ten years old, but Dad was good with machines. "You must be hungry."

"Not really," I said. I hadn't been hungry in a while. I hadn't cried in a while. Mostly I just felt numb.

"You should eat." He glanced at me as he pulled out of the parking lot. His lenses had become transparent, and behind them, his eyes were a flat, almost greyish brown. "There's a diner close to the apartment. If we get there now we'll have the place to ourselves."

"That's nice." Dad had never been social, but a little voice in my head said he didn't want to be seen with me. I took a deep breath. "Your glasses are cool."

"Oh?" He shrugged. "Astigmatism got worse. These help."

"It's good that you got it treated," I said, my words as staggered and awkward as I felt. I looked down at my lap.

"You've got my eyes, you know. You should take care of yourself."

"Yes, sir."

"We'll take you to the optometrist soon. Need to get your eye looked at after that shiner anyway…"

"Yes, sir." A billboard rose from the trees to the left, depicting a cartoon soldier firing red, white and blue sparks from a bazooka. GENERAL BLAMMO'S FIREWORK SHACK. We turned into the sun so his eyes were hidden again, his jaw set in a way I didn't know how to read. "What did Mom tell you?"

"She was worried about you," he said. "She said you weren't safe where you were living."

IF I WAS YOUR GIRL – OUT NOW

Praise for
IF I WAS *your* GIRL

"So powerful and poignant... I honestly just think this book will change a lot of people's lives."
Zoe Sugg

"*If I Was Your Girl* is important and necessary and brave, and deeply, electrically inspiring."
Jennifer Niven, New York Times bestselling author of
All the Bright Places

"Meredith Russo's debut is poignant and rare. *If I Was Your Girl* is the type of book you read and want to immediately share, because it's too important to keep to yourself."
Julie Murphy, #1 New York Times bestselling author of *Dumplin'*

"*If I Was Your Girl* is real and raw and layered and wonderful."
Alex Gino, author of *George*

"This book will change minds and open hearts."
Nina Lacour, Printz Award-winning author of *We Are Okay*

"A coming-of-age with real world gravitas and a love story with heart. Will not only keep readers hooked, it will make the world a better, more empathetic place."
Adi Alsaid, author of *Let's Get Lost*

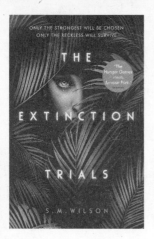
ONLY THE STRONGEST WILL BE CHOSEN
ONLY THE RECKLESS WILL SURVIVE

THE
EXTINCTION
TRIALS

S. M. WILSON

"DEEPLY DISTURBING AND
CHILLINGLY GOOD."
— Elizabeth Wein
NEW YORK TIMES BESTSELLING AUTHOR OF
CODE NAME VERITY

MATT KILLEEN

ORPHAN
MONSTER
SPY

COSTA BOOK AWARDS
2018

THE DEADLIEST WEAPON
IS A GIRL WITH
NOTHING TO LOSE

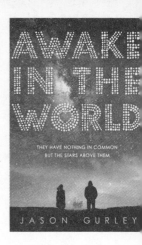
AWAKE
IN THE
WORLD

THEY HAVE NOTHING IN COMMON
BUT THE STARS ABOVE THEM

JASON GURLEY

Love this book? Love Usborne YA

Follow us online and sign up to the Usborne YA
newsletter for the latest YA books,
news and competitions:

usborne.com/yanewsletter

 @UsborneYA

"Genuinely different, thrilling an..."
Patrick Ness author of A MC...

AFTER
THE
FIRE

"Darkly fascinating...it's a must read novel"
Sarah Pinborough
author of BEHIND HER EYES

WILL HILL

HOLLY BOURNE

AM I
NORMAL
YET?

THE SPINSTER CLUB

"IMPORTANT AND BRAVE. READ THIS WONDERFUL
BOOK. JUST READ IT." JENNIFER NIVEN
Author of All the Bright Places

IF I WAS
your
GIRL

by MEREDITH RUSSO